Literature & Thought

To Be a Hero

Perfection Learning

EDITORIAL DIRECTOR   Julie A. Schumacher

SENIOR EDITOR   Terry Ofner

EDITOR   Linda Mazunik

PERMISSIONS   Laura Pieper
Lisa Lorimor

REVIEWERS   Mary Gershon
Lynne Albright
Ann Tharnish

DESIGN AND PHOTO RESEARCH
Jan Michalson
Lisa Lorimor

COVER ART LIFE LINE (detail) 1884 Winslow Homer
Philadelphia Museum of Art, George W. Elkins Collection

ACKNOWLEDGMENTS

"Birdfoot's Grampa" from *Entering Onondaga* © 1975 by Joseph Bruchac.

"Boy, Do We Ever Need a Hero" by David Granger. First published in *Esquire*, November 1998. Reprinted courtesy of *Esquire* and the Hearst Corporation.

"A Couple of Really Neat Guys" by Dave Barry. © Tribune Media Services, Inc. All Rights Reserved. Reprinted with permission.

"Dr. Martin Luther King, Jr." by David Dinkins. Reprinted by permission of the author.

"Elizabeth Blackwell: Medical Pioneer" by Joanna Kraus. Reprinted by permission of New Plays Incorporated. "Elizabeth Blackwell: Medical Pioneer" is a portion of a complete play, *Ms. Courageous: Women of Science*, available from New Plays Incorporated, P.O. Box 5074, Charlottesville, VA 22905.

CONTINUED ON PAGE 151

WHAT MAKES A HERO?

The question above is the *essential question* that you will consider as you read this book. The literature, activities, and organization of the book will lead you to think critically about this question and to develop a deeper understanding of heroes.

To help you shape your answer to the broad essential question, you will read and respond to four sections, or clusters. Each cluster addresses a specific question and thinking skill.

CLUSTER ONE What are some types of heroes? **CLASSIFYING**

CLUSTER TWO What makes a hero? **ANALYZING**

CLUSTER THREE Hero or not? **EVALUATING**

CLUSTER FOUR Thinking on your own **SYNTHESIZE**

Notice that the final cluster asks you to think independently about your answer to the essential question—*What makes a hero?*

To Be a Hero

A Song of Greatness

Chippewa Traditional

When I hear the old men
Telling of heroes,
Telling of great deeds
Of ancient days—
When I hear that telling,
Then I think within me
I, too, am one of these.
When I hear the people
Praising great ones,
Then I know that I too—
Shall be esteemed;
I, too, when my time comes
Shall do mightily.

Table of Contents

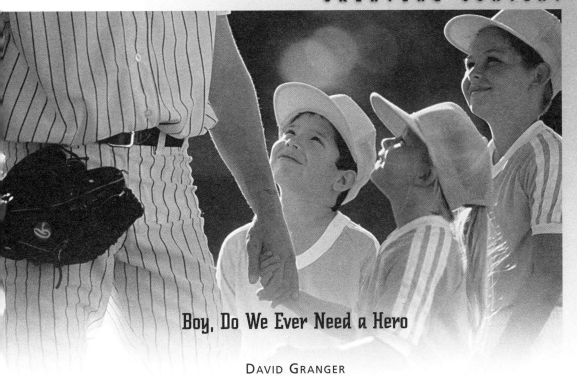

Boy, Do We Ever Need a Hero

DAVID GRANGER

It's corny, isn't it? Hero?

The notion, in this day and age, that there could be heroes? Heroes are for kids. Heroes are for youngsters. We're far too old and far too sophisticated to need heroes. Heroes are those things in the thirty- and sixty-second spots on the television, selling shoes. Or they're the heartwarming rescuers of cats whom the attractive anchorperson uses to fill in the odd moments between the mayhem[1] and the sexual misconduct and the weather. And if you do find heroes, when you hold them up to the light and study them—really study them—they're all flawed anyway.

But, boy, do we ever need a hero.

There are no heroes anymore. We can't find them. We certainly can't look for them in any of the places where we used to find them. There's no frontier anymore, and no New Frontier, and no Final Frontier, either, that we as a nation have pledged to explore and conquer. War is now fought from great distances, by shadow enemies. There is no iron curtain, no Red menace, and, God willing, no titanic struggle to save democracy. All our advances are small, in nanos and bytes, and heroes can't be small.

1 **mayhem:** damage or violence

But, boy, do we ever need a hero.

Even some of our heroes don't believe in heroes. A few months ago, I wrote to about two hundred people, asking them to name their heroes. We heard back from a great number of them, even if the response was simply to tell us that they weren't sure what the word meant. (We also asked an entire class of first graders, and only two had an idea of what the word meant.) One of the letters we got was from Paul Newman, who has himself lived a noble and generous life. He wrote: "I'm embarrassed, but I have no heroes that I know of. Everybody that I know or have read about is seriously flawed. Including myself." Mr. Newman did end up proposing his dog Harry as at least a good role model: "Funky, curious, always of good humor."

Boy, do we ever need a hero.

Seriously flawed. Deconstructing[2] heroes has become, or perhaps always was, a great American pasttime. It is, I suppose, healthy in some ways, but the obsessive discovery that goes on in this open society of ours has also put heroes on the endangered-species list. Seriously flawed? Depending on whom you ask, all of our proposed heroes are seriously flawed. Role models? Maybe. Idols? No. Just people who met their moment and sometimes left us speechless at what a human being is capable of.

Boy, do we need a hero.

Heroes arrive when we need them most. They define us and point us in a direction. To turn our sights at this moment toward an idea of America that is heroic does, admittedly, require an act of will. Well, our country has been nothing if not an act of will. To begin a redefinition of the American hero . . . is an act of will that says that whatever else we may actually *be,* it's to this that we aspire.[3] And as long as we need examples of how to live, as long as we aspire, we will never be too old for heroes. ∾

2 **deconstructing**: analyzing and criticizing
3 **aspire**: seek to reach a goal

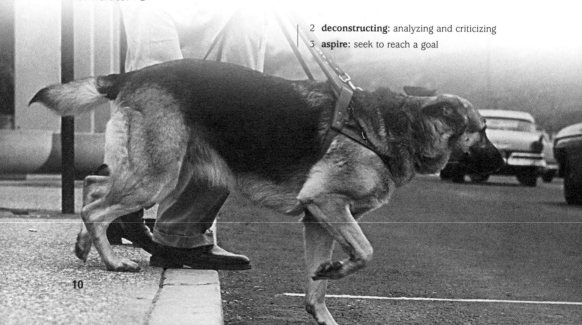

CONCEPT VOCABULARY

You will find the following terms and definitions useful as you read and discuss the selections in this book.

antagonist an adversary or opponent of a protagonist or hero

anti-hero the protagonist of a story who lacks generally accepted heroic qualities

champion warrior, fighter, or first-place winner

chivalry code of honorable conduct for medieval knights

courage strength to overcome fears, dangers, or difficulties

cowardice lack of courage

defender one who protects others, often by driving away danger or attack

gallantry acts of courage or bravery

hero a figure whom others admire for his or her noble conduct, achievements, or qualities; *heroine* sometimes used for female hero

ideal standard of excellence

inspiration moving a person's emotions or thoughts to a positive end

mentor a guide, coach, or person that others follow

model ideal pattern to imitate

paragon a supreme model set up as a comparison or inspiration

perseverence persisting in spite of obstacles

protagonist a main character in a piece of literature

redeemer a person who wins back or frees another from a dilemma

titan word taken from the name of a mythological giant; used now for one who stands out for great achievement or character

valor courage

victor winner or conqueror

CLUSTER ONE

What Are Some Types of Heroes?
Thinking Skill CLASSIFYING

Older Run

GARY PAULSEN

"**H**elp."

It was, in an impossible situation on an impossible night in an impossible life, the only possible thing to say.

I had never been in such an untenable,[1] completely bizarre situation.

The night had started easy, ridiculously easy, and I should have taken warning from the ease. Generally, when running dogs and sleds, a good moment or two will be followed by eight or nine hours of panic and disaster.

It was early on in training Cookie's pups. They were already trained, knew how to run, where to run, when to run and were having a ball. I was still in that phase of my life when I thought I had some semblance of control over the team, did not yet understand that the dogs ran the show—all of it—and, if I was extremely lucky and didn't hit a tree, I was allowed to hang on the back of the sled and be a spectator. The problem was that my education was coming so slowly that I had fallen behind the dogs—say a couple of years—and it was becoming very difficult to keep up.

This night had begun cleanly, wonderfully. It was midwinter, clear, fifteen or twenty below, a full moon—absolutely beautiful. I put Cookie on the front end and took three of the seasoned dogs and six of the pups, a total of ten dogs, counting Cookie.

Exceeding seven dogs was risky—more than seven dogs meant it would be difficult to stop them or control them, in fact it could not be done unless they wanted to stop—but I knew that and loaded the sled heavily with gear and four fifty-pound sacks of dog meat to help me control them.

---

1 **untenable:** unable to be defended or explained

Cookie held the gang line[2] out while I harnessed the rest of them, the pups last because they were so excited they kept jumping over the gang line and getting tangled, and when I popped the quick-release holding the sled to a post near the kennel we snapped out in good order.

That's how I thought of it—almost in a stuffy English manner. *Ahh yes, we left the kennel in good order, everything quite, that is to say, quite properly lined up.*

The weight of the sled did not seem to bother them at all. This, of course, should have been a warning to me, a caution that I had exceeded my limits of ability and understanding, but it was a smashing night (still in the English mode), clear and quite, that is to say, quite beautiful, and I gave them their head[3] (as if I had any choice).

We climbed the shallow hills out back of the kennel and moved into the forest. I had a plan to run a hundred miles—take twelve, fourteen hours with a rest stop—and see how the young dogs did with a slightly longer run. They had been to fifty twice and I didn't anticipate any difficulty. If they did get tired, I would just stop for a day and play—God knows I was carrying enough extra food.

I also decided to make it an "open" run and stay away from thick forests or winding trails. Young dogs tend to forget themselves in the excitement and sometimes run into trees on tight corners because they don't remember to swing out. It doesn't hurt them much, but it isn't pleasant and running should, of all things, be fun for them.

So I took the railroad grades. In northern Minnesota there used to be trains through the forests for hauling wood and supplies to the logging camps and to service the hundreds of small towns. Most of the towns are gone now, and much of the wood is hauled on trucks, but the railroad grades are still there.

In a decision so correct it seems impossible that government could have made it, they decided to pull the tracks and ties off the embankments and maintain them for wilderness trails. In the summer they use them for bicycles and hikers, in the winter for skiers and snowmobilers and now dogsledders.

The trails make for classic runs. It's possible to leave the kennel and run a week, hundreds and hundreds of miles, without seeing the same country twice.

2 **gang line:** line of dogs harnessed for running a sled
3 **gave them their head:** let them have their way

The one problem is the trestles. Minnesota is a land of lakes and rivers and every eight or ten miles the trains would cross a river. They made wooden trestles for the tracks and the trestles are still there. They are open, some of them sixty or seventy feet high, and bare wood—although they took the tracks themselves off so it was possible to see down through the ties.

Because they were open they would not hold snow so the snowmobile clubs covered them with one-inch treated plywood to close them in and provide a base for the snow.

The first few times we crossed one, the dogs hesitated, especially on the higher ones, but I took it easy and the older dogs figured it out and passed confidence to the team and it worked all right.

We had by this time run the trestles many times, knew where each one was, and the dogs whizzed across when we came to them.

Until now.

Twenty-five miles into the run, smoking through the moonlight, we came to a trestle over an open rushing river. I had turned my headlamp off to let them run in the moonlight, which they preferred, and was thinking ahead, way ahead, of a place we were going to camp to rest the pups. It was one of the most beautiful places I had ever seen, a quiet brook kept open by small warm springs, winding through a stand of elegant spruce and tall Norway pines. It was a place to make you whisper and think of churches, and I liked to stop there and sit by a fire, and I was thinking of how it would be to camp there and be peaceful when the dogs suddenly stopped.

. Dead in the middle of the trestle.

I hit the brake with my right foot and almost killed myself. Some maniac had come and stolen all the plywood from the trestle and when I jammed the two hardened steel teeth of the brake down instead of sliding on the plywood surface to a gradual stop, they caught on an open cross tie and stopped the sled instantly.

I, however, did not stop.

In a maneuver that would have looked right in an old Mack Sennett comedy,[4] I slammed into the cross handlebar with my stomach, drove all the wind out of my lungs, flew up and over the sled in a cartwheel, hit to the right of the wheel dogs, bounced once on the iron-hard cross ties of

---

4 **Mack Sennett comedy:** humorous movies from the early 1900s

the trestle, ricocheted[5] neatly into space, and dropped twenty feet into a snowbank next to the river, headfirst, driving in like a falling arrow.

All of this occurred so fast I couldn't mentally keep up with it and still somehow thought that I must be on the sled when I was upside down in the snowbank. As it was I had hit perfectly. Had I gone a few feet farther I would have landed in the river and probably have drowned or frozen, ten feet sooner and I would have missed the snowbank and hit bare packed ice, which would have broken my neck. It was the only place for me to land and not kill myself, but at the moment I was having trouble feeling gratitude.

I pushed my way out of the snow, cleared my eyes—it had happened so fast I hadn't had time to close them and they were full of snow—and peered up at the underside of the trestle where I could look through the ties and see the team still standing there, the dogs balanced precariously, teetering over open space.

"Easy," I called up. "Just easy now. Easy, easy, easy . . ."

Cookie had hit the trestle without stopping and run out, thinking that's what I wanted, until the whole team was out on the open ties. What stopped her was the pups. Somehow the adult dogs had kept up, stepping on ties as fast as possible to keep going, but the young dogs had less experience and had tripped and gone down. Thank heaven they weren't injured and Cookie stopped when she felt them fall.

But the problem was still there. The team was spread along the trestle, each dog on a tie, and it seemed an impossible situation. To swing a dog team around requires a great deal of space. If they are dragged back on top of each other they get dreadfully tangled and tend to fight, and I couldn't imagine a dogfight at night with ten dogs on a narrow railroad trestle twenty feet off the ground.

An answer did not come to me immediately. I climbed the bank back up onto the trestle. Cookie was frozen out in front of the team holding them, her back legs jammed against one cross tie and her front feet clawed on the one in front, and the snow hook had fallen in the impact of the stop and had set itself in the ties under the sled so the team was held in place while I decided what to do.

I couldn't turn them around.

I couldn't drive them over the trestle without injuring dogs.

"I can't do anything," I said aloud to Cookie, who was looking back at

---

5 **ricocheted:** bounced or glanced off the surface

me waiting for me to solve the thing. "It's impossible . . ."

You, her eyes said, *got us into this, and you'd better get us out.*

Her message hung that way for half a minute, my thoughts whirling, and I finally decided the only way to do it was to release each dog, one at a time, and let them go forward or backward on their own. I thought briefly of carrying them out, one by one, but I had no extra rope to tie them (it was the last run I made without carrying extra rope) when I got across the trestle.

I would have to let them go.

I started with the older dogs. I let them loose and set them on the ties and was amazed to see that each of them went on across the trestle— the longer way—rather than turn and go back. They didn't hesitate but set out, moving carefully from tie to tie until they were across. Whereupon they didn't stop and instead, as I had feared, took off down the railroad grade. They had been here before and knew the way home. I let the young dogs go then and they were slower and more frightened, especially when they looked down, but as soon as they crossed they took off as well and vanished in the night as they tried to catch up with the rest of the dogs.

"Well," I said to Cookie. "It's you and me . . ."

I let her loose and was amazed to see her take off after the team. We were good friends, had been for years, and I was sure she would stay with me, but she was gone in an instant.

"*Traitor.*" I said it with great feeling. The truth is she could not have pulled the sled anyway. It was too heavy for one dog. But it would have been nice to have company. I worried that they would have trouble, get injured somehow, run out on a highway and get hit by a car.

It was like watching my body leave me, my family, and I gathered up the gang line and unhooked the snow hook and dragged the sled across the trestle. Once I got it on the snow it slid a bit easier and I thought that it must be thirty, thirty-five miles to home the shortest way and it would take me three days—or three miserable days, as I considered it then. I had a thermos of tea on the sled and I took time to have a cup, feeling at intervals sorry for myself and hoping silently that I would someday meet the man who stole the plywood from the trestle.

I was putting the inevitable off and I finally accepted it and put away the thermos and moved to the front of the sled and put the gang line around my waist and started pulling. Once I broke it free it slid well enough and I set a slow pace. I had thought of hiding the sled in some way and coming back for it later but it was coming on a weekend and the snowmobilers would be on the trails and there were hundreds of them. Surely the sled—boiled white ash and oak with plastic runner shoes—would be too tempting.

I pulled half an hour on the embankment, trudging along—it seemed like a week—and I developed an updated gratitude for the dogs; their effortless strides covered miles so fast that I felt like with my own puny efforts I was on a treadmill. It seemed to take ten minutes to pass a tree.

Fifteen more minutes, I thought, *then I'll take a break.* I had also decided to throw out some of the dog food and let the wolves have it. It was commercial meat and had cost money but at the rate I was moving I wouldn't get it home until I was an old man anyway.

Ten minutes passed and I said to heck with it and sat down on the sled and was sitting there, sipping half a cup of tea, when I heard a sound and Minto, a large red dog who had a pointed face, came trotting up and sat down facing me.

"Hello," I said. "Get lonely?"

He cocked his head and I petted him, and while rubbing his ears another dog, named Winston, trotted up.

"What is this?" I asked. "Loyalty?"

The truth is they shouldn't have been there. I had lost dogs several times and had them leave me and run home. Trapline teams, or teams that are lived with and enjoyed recreationally, sometimes are trained to stay with the musher; and indeed Cookie had brought a team to me when I was injured once while trapping. But that is rare. Mostly they go home. And race teams, trained for only one thing, to go and go and never stop, simply do not come back. These were not trapline dogs but race dogs, and while I sat marveling at them four more came back, then one more, then the last two pups and, finally, Cookie.

I stood and spread out the gang line and hooked up their harnesses, which were still on the dogs, putting Cookie in first and then the rest, and I wanted to say something and I finally did manage to get "thank you" out. But in truth I couldn't speak. I had a lump the size of a softball in my throat. I stood on the back of the sled and they lined out and took off and I still wondered how it could be.

I do not know what happened out there—although some of the dogs had slight wounds in the end of their ears clearly made by bites. I did not see nor could I even guess what had transpired.

I know how it looked. I had been alone, Cookie had run after them,

and they had come back. All of them, some bleeding slightly from bitten ears. They all got in harness and we finished the run in good order and when I was sitting in the kitchen later, sipping a cup of hot soup and try-ing to explain it to Ruth, I shook my head.

"I know it sounds insane but it looked like Cookie went after them, caught them, and sent them back to me. I've never heard of anything like it."

"Well, if it looks like a duck, quacks like a duck, and walks like a duck . . ."

I nodded. "I agree, but it's so incredible."

"I don't know about that, but I do know one thing."

"What's that?"

"You aren't paying her nearly enough . . ." ❧

Wreckage from Air Florida Flight 90 pulled from the Potomac River, 1982.

The Man in the Water

ROGER ROSENBLATT

On January 13, 1982, Air Florida Flight 90 plowed into the 14th Street Bridge in Washington, D.C., and plunged into the frigid waters of the Potomac River. The plane hit seven vehicles, killing four motorists and 74 passengers. Only six people survived. This is one passenger's story.

As disasters go, this one was terrible but not unique, certainly not among the worst on the roster of U.S. air crashes. There was the unusual element of the bridge, of course, and the fact that the plane clipped it at a moment of high traffic, one routine thus intersecting another and disrupting both. Then, too, there was the location of the event. Washington, the city of form and regulations, turned chaotic, deregulated, by a blast of real winter and a single slap of metal on metal. The jets from Washington National Airport that normally swoop around the presidential monuments like famished gulls are, for the moment, emblemized by the one that fell; so there is that detail. And there was the aesthetic clash as well—blue-and-green Air Florida, the name a flying garden, sunk down among gray chunks in a black river. All that was worth noticing, to be sure. Still, there was nothing very special in any of it, except death, which, while always special, does not necessarily bring millions to tears or to attention. Why, then, the shock here?

Perhaps because the nation saw in this disaster something more than a mechanical failure. Perhaps because people saw in it no failure at all, but rather something successful about their makeup. Here, after all, were two forms of nature in collision: the elements and human character. Last Wednesday, the elements, indifferent as ever, brought down Flight 90. And on that same afternoon, human nature—groping and flailing in mysteries of its own—rose to the occasion.

Of the four acknowledged heroes of the event, three are able to account for their behavior. Donald Usher and Eugene Windsor, a park police helicopter team, risked their lives every time they dipped the skids into the water to pick off survivors. On television, side by side in bright blue jumpsuits, they described their courage as all in the line of duty. Lenny Skutnik, a 28-year-old employee of the Congressional Budget Office, said: "It's something I never thought I would do"–referring to his jumping into the water to drag an injured woman to shore. Skutnik added that "somebody had to go in the water," delivering every hero's line that is no less admirable for its repetitions. In fact, nobody had to go into the water. That somebody actually did so is part of the reason this particular tragedy sticks in the mind.

But the person most responsible for the emotional impact of the disaster is the one known at first simply as "the man in the water." (Balding, probably in his 50s, an extravagant mustache.) He was seen clinging with five other survivors to the tail section of the airplane. This man was described by Usher and Windsor as appearing alert and in control. Every time they lowered a lifeline and floating ring to him, he passed it on to another of the passengers. "In a mass casualty, you'll find people like him," said Windsor, "But I've never seen one with that commitment." When the helicopter came back for him the man had gone under. His selflessness was one reason the story held national attention; his anonymity another. The fact that he went unidentified invested him with a universal character. For a while he was Everyman, and thus proof (as if one needed it) that no man is ordinary.

Still, he could never have imagined such a capacity in himself. Only minutes before his character was tested, he was sitting in the ordinary plane among the ordinary passengers, dutifully listening to the stewardess telling him to fasten his seat belt and saying something about the "no smoking sign." So our man relaxed with the others, some of whom would owe their lives to him. Perhaps he started to read, or to doze, or to regret some harsh remark made in the office that morning. Then suddenly he knew that the trip would not be ordinary. Like every other person on that flight, he was desperate to live, which makes his final act so stunning.

For at some moment in the water he must have realized that he would not live if he continued to hand over the rope and ring to others. He *had* to know it, no matter how gradual the effect of the cold. In his judgment he had no choice. When the helicopter took off with what was to be the last survivor, he watched everything in the world move away from him, and he deliberately let it happen.

Yet there was something else about the man that kept our thoughts on him and which keeps our thoughts on him still. He was *there,* in the essential, classic circumstance. Man in nature. The man in the water. For its part, nature cared nothing about the five passengers. Our man, on the other hand, cared totally. So the timeless battle commenced in the Potomac. For as long as that man could last, they went at each other, nature and man: the one making no distinctions of good and evil, acting on no principles, offering no lifelines; the other acting wholly on distinctions, principles and, one supposes, on faith.

Since it was he who lost the fight, we ought to come again to the conclusion that people are powerless in the world. In reality, we believe the reverse, and it takes the act of the man in the water to remind us of our true feelings in this matter. It is not to say that everyone would have acted as he did or as Usher, Windsor and Skutnik. Yet whatever moved these men to challenge death on behalf of their fellows is not peculiar to them. Everyone feels the possibility in himself. That is the abiding wonder of the story. That is why we would not let go of it. If the man in the water gave a lifeline to the people gasping for survival, he was likewise giving a lifeline to those who observed him.

The odd thing is that we do not even really believe that the man in the water lost his fight. "Everything in Nature contains all the powers of Nature," said Emerson. Exactly. So the man in the water had his own natural powers. He could not make ice storms or freeze the water until it froze the blood. But he could hand life over to a stranger, and that is a power of nature too. The man in the water pitted himself against an implacable, impersonal enemy; he fought it with charity; and he held it to a standoff. He was the best we can do. ✍

Collage for the cover of the book *Minotaure*.
1933
Pablo Picasso

The Hero's Test

ALISOUN WITTING

Theseus had not been in Athens more than six months, learning the duties of a king from his father Aegeus, when his courage was tested. One bright spring morning, when all the world seemed new and alive, the people of Athens appeared strangely sad and gloomy, and the sound of women weeping came from many of the houses. Theseus was puzzled: what was the cause of this public sorrow? He asked his father; Aegeus hesitated, seemed embarrassed, and finally made some lame excuse about a festival of the dead. "If I cannot get the truth from my own father," he thought indignantly, "I will find it out from the common people." So he stopped the first citizen who passed him in the street, saying "Sir, tell me why my father's people mourn and appear sorrowful, in this season of joy and new birth."

The man stared at him.

"Why, have you not heard of the tribute[1] to King Minos?" he exclaimed. "He is the ruler of the Island of Crete, and he is the most powerful sea-king in the world. From every Greek city he demands a yearly tribute of seven boys and seven girls—and now the Cretan[2] ship has anchored in the harbor, and will sail with our children tomorrow."

Theseus stood silent with amazement.

"And what happens to the fourteen boys and girls?" he managed to ask at last.

"It is too terrible to say," the man said, shuddering. "If you were not

---

1 **tribute:** expected payment
2 **Cretan:** from the island of Crete off the coast of Greece

the king's own son, you might be chosen yourself—you are just the right age for the Minotaur."

"Who is the Minotaur?" demanded Theseus sharply, growing more and more angry at the story he was hearing.

The man trembled. "He is a dreadful beast, half bull and half man, who lives on human flesh. King Minos keeps him underground in a labyrinth[3] of twisting passages, where he is fed yearly on our Greek sons and daughters." He covered his face with his hands. "Oh Prince Theseus, do not ask me any more. My own children are still too young; but in a few years I too must place their names in the lot, and perhaps see one or more of them sent to Crete for sacrifice." And he wept with grief and horror at the thought.

Theseus nearly exploded with rage. "How can my father allow this to happen!" he cried in fury. "Has he no pride?—I can well see why he was ashamed to tell me this disgraceful thing!"

"Theseus, you are young, but you should not speak foolishly," the man said sternly. "Your father is not at fault; even Zeus, father of gods and men, allows this outrage to continue. Minos is powerful enough to destroy Athens in a day if we refuse him his tribute. We are no happier about it than you are, but there is nothing else we can do."

"There is!" declared Theseus passionately. "I will kill the Minotaur myself, and free Athens from this disgraceful tribute to Minos."

Full of his resolution he strode to the marketplace, where the young boys and girls of Athens were already gathered to be chosen by lot.

"Father," he said to Aegeus, "you were wrong not to tell me of this. A king must be responsible for his people; he must give his life for them, if necessary. You have no right to spare me because I am your son."

And turning to the marketplace he cried out in a ringing voice: "People of Athens, I myself volunteer to be one of the tribute to Crete. But I am not going to die unresisting, nor will I allow the Minotaur to slaughter your children unless he first kills me."

But the Athenians, far from being happy at this declaration, only protested that their handsome young prince should not rashly throw his life away in Crete, and leave them without a future ruler. Old Aegeus begged him to reconsider, to wait at least until he was full grown and might declare war on Minos. But Theseus had made up his mind, and his pride would not allow him to back down now, nor did he wish to.

3 **labyrinth:** a maze

"You are leaving me alone in my old age," cried Aegeus in grief and despair. "You foolishly desert your people when they most need a young king! Do not go to Crete, Theseus; for my sake, if not for your own, stay in Athens."

No use; he could not move Theseus. The next morning Aegeus, like thirteen other Athenian fathers, kissed his son in farewell, fully expecting never to see him again. But at the last minute he made Theseus promise one thing: if he should live, to return home under a white sail; if he died, to send the ship back with black sails.

The palace of Minos was huge. It covered acres of ground, a jumble of shining roofs and towers, walls and gates. Underneath his magnificent structure, deeper than the deepest basement, at the very foundation of the palace itself, lived the Minotaur. The labyrinth had a thousand twisting passages, a thousand rooms, and just as many dead ends. Through this maze roamed the frightful beast, whose body was shaped like a man's, and whose horned head was that of a bull. From time to time he gave a tremendous bellow, and his roaring shook the palace and the very ground beneath the city of Cnossus.[4] His victims were led into the labyrinth and left to their fate. They never succeeded in finding their way back to the entrance of the maze, for there were just too many confusing tunnels and passages; and so, one by one, the Minotaur found and ate them. Sometimes they lived for days before they were discovered, sometimes only a few hours. Imagine the terror of a boy or girl left to wander in this awful place, expecting at every turn and every opening to meet the savage Minotaur!

But Theseus was not easily frightened. Arriving at Cnossus, he and his companions were presented to King Minos for approval before they were sacrificed. The young hero stood out among his companions like an oak among pine trees, and he appeared so noble that Minos' daughter, the beautiful princess Ariadne, fell deeply in love with him. That night in her pretty room, decorated with painted dolphins and graceful sea-creatures, she wept for hours to think of Theseus' terrible fate. At length she sat up, dried her eyes, wrapped herself in a dark cloak, and slipped out of her room. She ran softly through the long corridors of the palace, past the drowsy sentries,[5] until she reached the cell where the Athenians were imprisoned.

---

4 **Cnossus:** ancient center of the Minoan civilization on Crete's north central coastline

5 **sentries:** guards

The boys and girls slept soundly, for their wine had been drugged that night to make sure they were rested and alert when they were sent into the labyrinth. (The Minotaur preferred a little sport before his meals.) But Theseus had eaten little, and had quietly poured his wine between the stones of the prison floor, for he suspected the Cretan trick, and had good reasons to stay awake. He was planning his strategy for the next day, and wondering how, unarmed, he would be able to kill the Minotaur. Stones would be his only weapon, he thought, or perhaps a bone from the Minotaur's former feasts. Theseus shivered in spite of himself. Then he saw Ariadne. She stood pressed behind a pillar, so close to the bars that when he stood beside them he could almost touch her.

"Theseus," she whispered, "listen closely. Tomorrow at the entrance to the labyrinth you will find an axe and a ball of string. With the axe you will have a chance to kill the Minotaur; with the string you may find your way back out of the maze." Theseus opened his mouth to thank her but the sentry nearby moved and coughed, and they both pressed into the shadows and held their breath. When the guard was quiet again Ariadne said quickly, "Goodby. If you live, remember me—I love you, Theseus." And she was gone, as swiftly and silently as she had come. As for Theseus, he lay down and slept soundly for the rest of that night.

Early the next morning the fourteen Athenians were awakened and dressed in white robes for their sacrifice. Then they were led, by the light of torches, down great flights of stone stairs, deep into the heart of the earth to the entrance of the labyrinth. Presently they stood trembling before a huge bronze door, which the guard unlocked with a great key. He shoved them in hastily—for he himself was afraid of an unexpected appearance of the Minotaur—thrust a torch into a bracket on the wall, and slammed the mighty door behind them. They heard the key turn smoothly in the lock and his footsteps retreating up the stone steps, and then they were quite alone in the gloomy cavern, with the torchlight dancing in weird shadows on the rough stone walls. Theseus alone did not give way to tears and panic. He looked closely about the doorway and sure enough, there was a large ball of stout string, and a sharp, double-edged axe. He strapped the axe about his waist, took the torch in his left hand, and gave the end of the string to one of his companions. "Now be quiet," he warned the bewildered boys and girls. "Don't move from this spot, but pray to the gods that it is I, and not the Minotaur, who will be guided back by this string." And he set out to meet the bull-monster, unrolling Ariadne's string as he went.

The labyrinth twisted like the coils of a snake, or like the coils of many snakes hopelessly tangled together. Theseus walked along circular passages, up flights of steps, down holes. He ducked under little doorways, found himself suddenly in huge rooms, scrambled down tiny tunnels, and bumped into countless dead-end turns. But he carefully unrolled his string, kept hold of his sputtering torch, and prayed under his breath that he would meet the Minotaur in an open space where he could fight freely, and not in one of the damp, narrow passages. Often the air trembled from the deep growls and bellows of the Minotaur, and Theseus followed the sound, his heart pounding as each roar grew louder and nearer.

Then suddenly he stepped round a corner into a large hall. The ceiling was high and a row of small windows at the top of the walls cast a dim, ghostly light. The floor was covered with bones, and in the center of this horrible place stood the shaggy, bull-headed Minotaur himself. Theseus dropped his torch and the ball of string and snatched the axe from his belt, and not a moment too soon, either, for the Minotaur took just one look at him, let out a tremendous howl of rage and charged. Then a long battle began. The Minotaur was a huge, powerful beast, but the wits of his bull head were not very sharp, and his fighting tactics were limited to a fast charge, horns lowered. After five or six murderous charges which Theseus easily sidestepped, the Minotaur became confused and furious. He stood stamping and snorting and glared at his quick-footed enemy with bloodshot eyes. He tried to force Theseus into a corner, meaning to pin him to the wall. But Theseus was far too quick to be trapped, and half the time the monster could not even see where he had gone. Soon the Minotaur began to tire; Theseus danced around him, drawing him on, dodging, and tormenting him until the beast was foaming at the mouth and rushing half-blindly about. Now Theseus began to use his axe. As the Minotaur rushed by Theseus would swing and graze his hairy shoulder, or an arm, or his powerful back. The Minotaur's roars grew even louder and more savage at these wounds.

But Theseus was getting tired, too. He had been hopping about so long and so energetically that his legs were trembling with fatigue and his breath was coming in gasps. So when the Minotaur turned suddenly after a blind charge and rushed straight at him, Theseus had to jump so quickly that he stumbled backwards and nearly fell. Now the Minotaur was in close and Theseus was swinging the double-edged axe to defend his very life. Raising the axe over his head, he brought it down with all his force on the huge bull's forehead and split the Minotaur's skull between the horns. The axe-blow and the Minotaur's head were both so hard that the shock numbed Theseus' arms, and he fell exhausted against the wall as the monster spun around and toppled to the floor with a heavy thud. Theseus took the axe and chopped the Minotaur's head from his body. Then, finding Ariadne's string, he took one last look at the gruesome room and the dead Minotaur, and started back through the labyrinth.

He had to find his way in the dark this time, for his torch had gone out when he dropped it, and the way seemed very long. But the string guided him, and finally he could feel the pull of a human hand at the other end and hear the voices of his companions. The first person he saw was Ariadne, who cried out with joy and ran to embrace him. "We must leave here at once," she said fearfully. "It has been foretold that Cnossus will fall and the power of Minos be destroyed at the death of the Minotaur. Come quickly, Theseus, before my father's soldiers discover what you have done." She led them through the back ways of the palace and down a rocky footpath to the beach, where the Greek ship with its black sails was waiting, its sailors anxious to push off into the water.

When they were safely beyond the reach of Cretan ships, and the island itself was fading on the horizon, the Athenians were free to rejoice at their escape and to praise Theseus and Ariadne for their courage and love. They were, indeed, very much in love and overjoyed to be safe together, despite Theseus' weariness and Ariadne's sorrow at leaving her homeland. "I will make you my queen when we reach Athens," Theseus promised her.

The prophecy of the destruction of Cnossus was fulfilled that same day, for no sooner had the Greek ship dipped over the horizon than a mighty earthquake shook the island of Crete and tumbled the walls and towers of Minos' palace into heaps of rubble. King Minos himself was killed, most of his warships were sunk in the tidal wave that followed the earthquake, and the remains of the palace were burned by overturned oillamps and torches. So the sea-power of Crete was destroyed with the destruction of the Minotaur, and not just Athens but all the Greek cities were freed from the yearly tribute. ❧

Birdfoot's Grampa

JOSEPH BRUCHAC

The old man
must have stopped our car
two dozen times to climb out
and gather into his hands
the small toads blinded
by our light and leaping,
live drops of rain.

The rain was falling,
a mist about his white hair
and I kept saying
you can't save them all,
accept it, get back in
we've got places to go.

But, leathery hands full
of wet brown life,
knee deep in the summer
roadside grass,
he just smiled and said
they have places to go, too.

A portion of Nicholas Gage's third grade class; Nicholas Gage is in the middle of the top row; his sister Fotini is on the left in the second row from the bottom.

The Teacher Who Changed My Life

NICHOLAS GAGE

The person who set the course of my life in the new land I entered as a young war refugee—who, in fact, nearly dragged me onto the path that would bring all the blessings I've received in America—was a salty-tongued,[1] no-nonsense schoolteacher named Marjorie Hurd. When I entered her classroom in 1953, I had been to six schools in five years, starting in the Greek village where I was born in 1939.

When I stepped off a ship in New York Harbor on a gray March day in 1949, I was an undersized 9-year-old in short pants who had lost his mother and was coming to live with the father he didn't know. My mother, Eleni Gatzoyiannis, had been imprisoned, tortured and shot by Communist guerrillas for sending me and three of my four sisters to freedom. She died so that her children could go to their father in the United States.

The portly, bald, well-dressed man who met me and my sisters seemed a foreign, authoritarian figure. I secretly resented him for not getting the whole family out of Greece early enough to save my mother. Ultimately, I would grow to love him and appreciate how he dealt with becoming a single parent at the age of 56, but at first our relationship was prickly, full of hostility.

As Father drove us to our new home—a tenement[2] in Worcester, Massachusetts—and pointed out the huge brick building that would be our first school in America, I clutched my Greek notebooks from the refugee camp, hoping that my few years of schooling would impress my teachers

---

1 **salty-tongued:** lively talking, able to hold interesting conversations
2 **tenement:** apartment house

in this cold, crowded country. They didn't. When my father led me and my 11-year-old sister to Greendale Elementary School, the grim-faced Yankee principal put the two of us in a class for the mentally retarded. There was no facility in those days for non-English-speaking children.

By the time I met Marjorie Hurd four years later, I had learned English, been placed in a normal, graded class and had even been chosen for the college preparatory track in the Worcester public school system. I was 13 years old when our father moved us yet again, and I entered Chandler Junior High shortly after the beginning of seventh grade. I found myself surrounded by richer, smarter and better-dressed classmates, who looked askance at my strange clothes and heavy accent. Shortly after I arrived, we were told to select a hobby to pursue during "club hour" on Fridays. The idea of hobbies and clubs made no sense to my immigrant ears, but I decided to follow the prettiest girl in my class—the blue-eyed daughter of the local Lutheran minister. She led me through the door marked "Newspaper Club" and into the presence of Miss Hurd, the newspaper advisor and English teacher who would become my mentor and my muse.

A formidable, solidly built woman with salt-and-pepper hair, a steely eye and a flat Boston accent, Miss Hurd had no patience with layabouts. "What are all you goof-offs doing here?" she bellowed at the would-be journalists. "This is the Newspaper Club! We're going to put out a *news-paper*. So if there's anybody in this room who doesn't like work, I suggest you go across to the Glee Club now, because you're going to work your tails off here!"

I was soon under Miss Hurd's spell. She did indeed teach us to put out a newspaper, skills I honed during my next 25 years as a journalist. Soon I asked the principal to transfer me to her English class as well. There, she drilled us on grammar until I finally began to understand the logic and structure of the English language. She assigned stories for us to read and discuss; not tales of heroes, like the Greek myths I knew, but stories of underdogs—poor people, even immigrants, who seemed ordinary until a crisis drove them to do something extraordinary. She also introduced us to the literary wealth of Greece—giving me a new perspective on my war-ravaged, impoverished homeland. I began to be proud of my origins.

One day, after discussing how writers should write about what they know, she assigned us to compose an essay from our own experience. Fixing me with a stern look, she added, "Nick, I want you to write about what happened to your family in Greece." I had been trying to put those painful memories behind me and left the assignment until the last moment. Then, on a warm spring afternoon, I sat in my room with a yellow pad and pencil and stared out the window at the buds on the trees. I wrote that the coming of spring always reminded me of the last time I said goodbye to my mother on a green and gold day in 1948.

I kept writing, one line after another, telling how the Communist guerrillas occupied our village, took our home and food, how my mother started planning our escape when she learned that the children were to be sent to re-education camps behind the Iron Curtain and how, at the last moment, she couldn't escape with us because the guerrillas sent her with a group of women to thresh wheat in a distant village. She promised she would try to get away on her own, she told me to be brave and hung a silver cross around my neck, and then she kissed me. I watched the line of women being led down into the ravine and up the other side, until they disappeared around the bend—my mother a tiny brown figure at the end who stopped for an instant to raise her hand in one last farewell.

I wrote about our nighttime escape down the mountain, across the minefields and into the lines of the Nationalist soldiers, who sent us to a refugee camp. It was there that we learned of our mother's execution. I felt very lucky to have come to America, I concluded, but every year, the coming of spring made me feel sad because it reminded me of the last time I saw my mother.

Nicholas Gage and Miss Hurd

I handed in the essay, hoping never to see it again, but Miss Hurd had it published in the school paper. This mortified me at first, until I saw that my classmates reacted with sympathy and tact to my family's story. Without telling me, Miss Hurd also submitted the essay to a contest sponsored by the Freedoms Foundation at Valley Forge, Pennsylvania, and it won a medal. The Worcester paper wrote about the award and quoted my essay at length. My father, by then a "five-and-dime-store chef," as the paper described him, was ecstatic with pride, and the Worcester Greek community celebrated the honor to one of its own.

▲ ▲ ▲

For the first time I began to understand the power of the written word. A secret ambition took root in me. One day, I vowed, I would go back to Greece, find out the details of my mother's death and write about her life, so her grandchildren would know of her courage. Perhaps I would even track down the men who killed her and write of their crimes. Fulfilling that ambition would take me 30 years.

Meanwhile, I followed the literary path that Miss Hurd had so forcefully set me on. After junior high, I became the editor of my school paper at Classical High School and got a part-time job at the Worcester *Telegram and Gazette*. Although my father could only give me $50 and encouragement toward a college education, I managed to finance four years at Boston University with scholarships and part-time jobs in journalism. During my last year of college, an article I wrote about a friend who had died in the Philippines—the first person to lose his life working for the Peace Corps[3]—led to my winning the Hearst Award for College Journalism. And the plaque was given to me in the White House by President John F. Kennedy.

For a refugee who had never seen a motorized vehicle or indoor plumbing until he was 9, this was an unimaginable honor. When the Worcester paper ran a picture of me standing next to President Kennedy, my father rushed out to buy a new suit in order to be properly dressed to receive the congratulations of the Worcester Greeks. He clipped out the photograph, had it laminated in plastic and carried it in his breast pocket for the rest of his life to show everyone he met. I found the much-worn photo in his pocket on the day he died 20 years later. ೲ

3 **Peace Corps:** an organization established in 1961 by President John F. Kennedy; American volunteers serve worldwide to promote peace and friendship through education, community development, agriculture, health care, and public works.

Flying in the Face of the Führer

PHIL TAYLOR

You were a child, a dark-skinned child, and you knew Jesse Owens before you even knew why. He had been a sprinter and a broad jumper, that much you understood; but there was something more than just his speed that made black folk, even people who cared nothing about sports, swell their chests a little bit at the mention of his name. There was this one time when your house was full, loud with laughter, and a distinguished-looking older man appeared on the television screen. "Isn't that Jesse?" somebody asked. "Hush, that's Jesse." And there was silence while Jesse Owens spoke.

He was in his 50s by then, and the young Owens, the one older people saw in their mind's eye, was a spectral[1] figure to you. Even after you understood what he had done, how he had mortified Adolf Hitler[2] by winning

1 **spectral:** ghostly
2 **Adolf Hitler:** German dictator

Luz Long and Jesse Owens
at the 1936 Olympics.

four gold medals in the 1936 Berlin Olympics, he seemed unreal, and that murky black-and-white newsreel of his Olympic performance only made him more so. As he raced past his competitiors he was more idea than man, a charcoal rebuttal[3] to Nazi notions of Aryan supremacy.[4]

You cannot truly say you wish you had been there in Berlin to see him win the broad jump and the 100- and 200-meter dashes, and run the first leg for the victorious 4 x 100-meter relay-team—not in that place at that time in history. Merely being in the stadium on those muggy August days would not have been enough to truly grasp the flesh and blood of it anyway. To do that you would have had to be down on the infield with him for the second event, the broad jump, in which his main competitor was one of Hitler's most prized athletes, Luz Long. Owens, the world-record holder in the event, had fouled on the first two of his three qualifying jumps. Now

3 **rebuttal:** argument to contradict an opposing view
4 **Nazi notions of Aryan supremacy:** Hitler's political party, the Nazis, believed in the rule of a "superior race" of non-Jewish people, or Aryans.

he was in a state of panic—his third jump would be his last chance to advance. Failure would not just humiliate him, it would also give credence[5] to the vile theories of Hitler, who, after Owens had won the 100, had said, "The Americans should be ashamed of themselves, letting Negroes win their medals for them. I shall not shake hands with this Negro."

It was after Owens's second foul in the broad jump that Long, of all people, approached him. "What has taken your goat?"[6] he asked, making Owens smile at the mangled American idiom.[7] They talked briefly, and Long offered words of encouragement and advice, suggesting that Owens start farther back on his approach to make sure he didn't foul. Calmed, Owens sailed past the qualifying distance on his third jump and later that day beat Long for the gold medal with a leap of 26' 5¼", then an Olympic record. The two men cemented their bond later in the Olympic Village, talking well into the night about athletics and art, about race and politics. Those were the moments you wish you could have witnessed, when two competitors of different races, with different allegiances, found common ground.

Owens returned to the U.S. a hero, but after the commotion died down, he was still a black man in the 1930s America. Less than a year after the Olympics, unable to find a job with both dignity and a paycheck big enough to pay his college tuition, he had to lower himself to racing exhibitions against horses three times a week. Five cents of every dollar people paid to watch the spectacle went into Owens's pocket. Even that couldn't diminish his stature in the eyes of people who remembered those days in Berlin. Nor could it diminish him in the eyes of a dark-skinned child who was told the tale.

Now there is another child, very much like the boy you once were, and he sees Owens's picture on the book in your hand. You ask him if he knows who Jesse Owens was, and he says he has heard the name. Now it is time to tell him why. ∾

---

5 **credence:** credit; support

6 **"What has taken your goat?":** Long meant to say, "What has gotten your goat?" meaning "What has made you upset?"

7 **idiom:** expression; saying

RESPONDING TO CLUSTER ONE

WHAT ARE SOME TYPES OF HEROES?

Thinking Skill CLASSIFYING

1. Using a web chart such as the one below, classify the heroes of this cluster. For example, you might classify Cookie of "Older Run" as a rescuer. You will have to come up with labels for other categories on your chart.

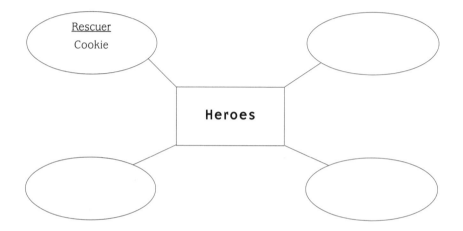

2. Do you think Theseus would have been a hero without Ariadne's help? Why or why not?

3. How many heroes can you find in "The Teacher Who Changed My Life"? Why do you consider them to be heroic?

4. Jesse Owens is the main hero in "Flying in the Face of the Führer." In what ways is Luz Long a hero too?

Writing Activity: Sketch a Hero

Think of a person or character you consider a hero. Is he or she a sports figure? A community leader? A teacher? What are the qualities of your ideal hero? Create a character sketch of this person.

A Strong Character Sketch

• describes a person's interests, traits, skills, mannerisms, personality, etc.

• paints a picture with words using strong descriptive language

• focuses on character traits that make the person unique

CLUSTER TWO

WHAT MAKES A HERO?
Thinking Skill   ANALYZING

Tough Alice

JANE YOLEN

The pig fell down the rabbit-hole, turning snout over tail and squealing as it went. By the third level it had begun to change. Wonderland was like that, one minute pig, the next pork loin.

It passed Alice on the fourth level, for contrary to the law of physics, she was falling much more slowly than the pig. Being quite hungry, she reached out for it. But no sooner had she set her teeth into its well-done flesh than it changed back into a live pig. Its squeals startled her and she dropped it, which made her use a word her mother had never even heard, much less understood. Wonderland's denizens[1] had done much for Alice's education, not all of it good.

"I promise I'll be a vegetarian if only I land safely," Alice said, crossing her fingers as she fell. At that very moment she hit bottom, landing awkwardly on top of the pig.

"Od-say off-ay!" the pig swore, swatting at her with his hard trotter.[2] Luckily he missed and ran right off toward a copse[3] of trees, calling for his mum.

"The same to you," Alice shouted after him. She didn't know what he'd said but guessed it was in Pig Latin. "You shouldn't complain, you know. After all, you're still whole!" Then she added softly, "And I can't complain, either. If you'd been a pork loin, I wouldn't have had such a soft landing." She had found over the years of regular visits that it was

1 **denizens:** inhabitants; citizens
2 **trotter:** pig's foot
3 **copse:** small thicket or grove of trees

ALICE BATTLES THE JABBERWOCK
1865
Sir John Tenniel

always best to praise Wonderland aloud for its bounty, however bizarre that bounty might be. You didn't want to have Wonderland mad at you. There were things like . . . the Jabberwock, for instance.

The very moment she thought the word, she heard the beast roar behind her. That was another problem with Wonderland. Think about something, and it appeared. *Or don't think about something*, Alice reminded herself, *and it still might appear*. The Jabberwock was her own personal Wonderland demon. It always arrived sometime during her visit, and someone—her chosen champion—had to fight it, which often signaled an end to her time there.

"Not so soon," Alice wailed in the general direction of the roar. "I haven't had much of a visit yet!" The Jabberwock sounded close, so Alice sighed and raced after the pig into the woods.

The woods had a filter of green and yellow leaves overhead, as lacy as one of her mother's parasols.[4] It really would have been quite lovely if Alice hadn't been in such a hurry. But it was best not to linger anywhere in Wonderland before the Jabberwock was dispatched. Tarrying simply invited disaster.

She passed the Caterpillar's toadstool. It was as big as her uncle Martin, and as tall and pasty white, but it was empty. A sign by the stalk said GONE FISHING. Alice wondered idly if the Caterpillar fished with worms, then shook her head. Worms would be too much like using his own family for bait. Though she had some relatives for whom that might not be a bad idea. Her cousin Albert, for example, who liked to stick frogs down the back of her dress.

Behind her the Jabberwock roared again.

"Bother!" said Alice, and began to zigzag through the trees.

"Haste . . ." came a voice from above her, "makes wastrels."[5]

Alice stopped and looked up. The Cheshire Cat's grin hung like a demented quarter moon between two limbs of an elm tree.

"Haste," continued the grin, "is a terrible thing to waste."

"That's really not quite right . . ." Alice began, but the grin went on without pausing:

"Haste is waste control. Haste is wasted on the young. Haste is . . ."

"You are in a loop," said Alice, and not waiting to hear another roar from the Jabberwock, ran on. Sunlight pleated down through the trees,

---

4 **parasols:** umbrellas used as sunshades

5 **wastrels:** foolish, wasteful persons

THE MAD HATTER
1865
Sir John Tenniel

wider and wider. Ahead a clearing beckoned. Alice could not help being drawn toward it.

In the center of the clearing a tea party was going on. Hatter to Dormouse to Hare, the conversation was thrown around the long oak table like some erratic ball in a game without rules. The Hatter was saying that teapots made bad pets and the Dormouse that teapots were big pests and the Hare that teapots held big tempests.

Alice knew that if she stopped for tea—chamomile would be nice, with a couple of wholemeal bisquits—the Jabberwock would . . .

ROAR!

. . . would be on her in a Wonderland moment. And she hadn't yet found a champion for the fight. So she raced past the tea table, waving her hand.

The tea-party trio did not even stop arguing long enough to call out her name. Alice knew from long experience that Wonderland friends were hardly the kind to send postcards or to remember your birthday, but she had thought they might at least wave back. After all the times she had poured for them, and brought them cakes from the Duchess's pantry! The last trip to Wonderland, she'd even come down the rabbit-hole with her pockets stuffed full of fruit scones[6] because the Dormouse had never tried them with currants.[7] He had spent the entire party after that making jokes about currant affairs, and the Hare had been laughing the whole time. "Hare-sterically," according to the Hatter. *We'd had a simply wonderful time*, Alice thought. It made her a bit cranky that the three ignored her now, but she didn't stop to yell at them or complain. The Jabberwock's roars were too close for that.

Directly across the clearing was a path. On some of her visits the path was there; on others it was twenty feet to the left or right. She raced toward it, hoping the White Knight would be waiting. He was the best of her champions, no matter that he was a bit old and feeble. At least he was always trying. *Quite trying,*[8] she thought suddenly.

She'd even settle for the Tweedle twins, though they fought one another as much as they fought the Jabberwock. Dee and Dum were their names, but—she thought a bit acidly—perhaps Dumb and Dumber more accurately described them.

And then there was the Beamish Boy. She didn't much like him at all, though he *was* the acknowledged Wonderland Ace. Renowned in song and story for beating the Jabberwock, he was too much of a bully for Alice's tastes. And he always insisted on taking the Jabberwock's head off with him. Even for Wonderland, *that* was a messy business.

Of course, this time, with the beast having gotten such an early start, Alice thought miserably, she might need them all. She had hoped for more time before the monster arrived on the scene. Wonderland was usually so much more fun than a vacation at Bath or Baden-Baden,[9] the one being her mother's favorite holiday spot, the other her grandmother's.

But when she got to the path, it was empty. There was no sign of the White Knight or the Tweedles or even the Beamish Boy, who—now that she thought of it—reminded her awfully of Cousin Albert.

6 **scones:** triangular-shaped bread

7 **currants:** seedless raisins

8 **trying:** severely straining one's patience

9 **Bath or Baden-Baden:** health resort towns known for their warm mineral springs; Bath in England and Baden-Baden in Germany

And suddenly the Jabberwock's roars were close enough to shake the trees. Green and gold leaves fell around her like rain.

Alice bit her lip. Wonderland might be only a make-believe place, a dreamscape, or a dream escape. But even in a made-up land, there were real dangers. She'd been hurt twice just falling down the rabbit-hole: a twisted ankle one time, a scratched knee another. And once she had pricked her finger on a thorn in the talking flower garden hard enough to draw blood. How the roses had laughed at that!

However, the Jabberwock presented a different kind of danger altogether. He was a horrible creature, nightmarish, with enormous shark-toothed jaws, claws like gaffing hooks,[10] and a tail that could swat her like a fly. There was no doubt in her mind that the Jabberwock could actually kill her if he wished, even in this imaginary land. He had killed off two of her champions on other visits—a Jack of Clubs and the Dodo—and had to be dispatched[11] by the Beamish Boy. She'd never seen either of the champions again.

The thought alone frightened her, and that was when she started to cry.

"No crying allowed," said a harsh, familiar voice.

"No crying aloud," said a quieter voice, but one equally familiar.

Alice looked up. The Red and White Queens were standing in front of her, the White Queen offering a handkerchief that was slightly tattered and not at all clean. "Here, blow!"

Alice took the handkerchief and blew, a sound not unlike the Jabberwock's roar, only softer and infinitely less threatening. "Oh," she said, "thank goodness you are here. You two can save me."

"Not us," said the Red Queen.

"Never us," added the White.

"But then why else have you come?" Alice asked. "I am always saved on this path . . . wherever this path is at the time."

"The path is past," said the Red Queen. "We are only present, not truly here." As she spoke the dirt path dissolved, first to pebbles, then to grass.

"And you are your own future," added the White Queen.

Alice suddenly found herself standing in the meadow once again, but this time the Hare, the Hatter, and the Dormouse were sitting in stands set atop the table. Next to them were the Caterpillar, his fishing pole over his shoulder; the Cheshire Cat, grinning madly; the White Knight; the Tweedle Twins;

---

10 **gaffing hooks:** large hooks for holding or lifting heavy fish
11 **dispatched:** disposed of

the Beamish Boy, in a bright red beanie;[12] the Duchess and her pig baby; and a host of other Wonderlanders. They were exchanging money right and left.

"My money's on you," the White Queen whispered in Alice's ear. "I think you will take the Jabberwock in the first round."

"Take him where?" asked Alice.

"For a fall," the Red Queen answered. Then, shoving a wad of money at the White Queen, she said, "I'll give you three to one against."

"Done," said the White Queen, and they walked off arm-in-arm toward the spectator stands, trailing bits of paper money on the ground.

"But what can I fight the Jabberwock with?" Alice called after them.

"You are a tough child," the White Queen said over her shoulder. "You figure it out."

With that she and the Red Queen climbed onto the table and into the stands, where they sat in the front row and began cheering, the White Queen for Alice, the Red Queen for the beast.

"But I'm not tough at all," Alice wailed. "I've never fought *anything* before. Not even Albert." She had only told on him, and had watched with satisfaction when her mother and his father punished him. Or at least that had seemed satisfactory at first. But when his three older sisters had all persisted in calling "Tattletale twit, your tongue will split" after her for months, it hadn't felt very satisfactory at all.

"I am only," she wept out loud, "a tattletale, not a knight."

"It's not night now!" shouted the Hatter.

"Day! It's day! A frabjous[13] day!" the Hare sang out.

The Beamish Boy giggled and twirled the propeller on the top of his cap.

Puffing five interlocking rings into the air above the crowd, the Caterpillar waved his arms gaily.

And the Jabberwock, with eyes of flame, burst out of the tulgey[14] wood, alternately roaring and burbling. It was a horrendous sound and for a moment Alice could not move at all.

"One, two!" shouted the crowd. "Through and through."

The Jabberwock lifted his tail and slammed it down in rhythm to the chanting. Every time his tail hit the ground, the earth shook. Alice could feel each tremor move up from her feet, through her body, till it seemed as if the top of her head would burst open with the force of the

---

12 **beanie:** round, tight-fitting cap

13 **frabjous:** nonsense adjective from Lewis Carroll's poem "Jabberwocky"

14 **tulgey:** another nonsense adjective from Carroll's poem

blow. She turned to run.

"She ain't got no vorpal[15] blade," cried the Duchess, waving a fist. "How's she gonna fight without her bloomin' blade?"

At her side, the pig squealed: "Orpal-vay ade-blay."

The Beamish Boy giggled once more.

Right! Alice thought. *I haven't a vorpal blade. Or anything else, for that matter.*

For his part, the Jabberwock seemed delighted that she was weaponless, and he stood up on his hind legs, claws out, to slash a right and then a left in Alice's direction.

All Alice could do was duck and run, duck and run again. The crowd cheered and a great deal more money changed hands. The Red Queen stuffed dollars, pounds, *lira,* and *kroner*[16] under her crown as fast as she could manage. On the other hand, the Dormouse looked into his teapot and wept.

"Oh, Alice," came a cry from the stands, "be tough, child. Be strong." It was the White Queen's voice. "You do not need a blade. You just need courage."

Courage, Alice thought, *would come much easier with a blade.* But she didn't say that aloud. Her tongue felt as if it had been glued by fear to the roof of her mouth. And her feet, by the Queen's call, to the ground.

And still the Jabberwock advanced, but slowly, as if he were not eager to finish her off all at once.

He is playing with me, Alice thought, *rather like my cat, Dinah.* It was not a pleasant thought. She had rescued many a mouse from Dinah's claws and very few of them had lived for more than a minute or two after. She tried to run again but couldn't.

Suddenly she'd quite enough of Wonderland.

But Wonderland was not quite done with Alice.

The Jabberwock advanced. His eyes lit up like skyrockets and his tongue flicked in and out.

"Oh, Mother," Alice whispered. "I am sorry for all the times I was naughty. Really I am." She could scarcely catch her breath, and she promised herself that she would try and die nobly, though she really didn't want to die at all. Because if she died in Wonderland, who would explain it to her family?

15 **vorpal:** yet another nonsense adjective from Carroll's poem

16 **pounds, lira, and kroner:** British, Italian, and Scandanavian units of money

The Jabberwock moved closer. He slobbered a bit over his pointed teeth. Then he slipped on a pound note, staggered like Uncle Martin after a party, and his big yellow eyes rolled up in his head. "Ouf," he said.

"Ouf?" Alice whispered. "Ouf?"

It had all been so horrible and frightening, and now, suddenly, it was rather silly. She stared at the Jabberwock and for the first time noticed a little tag on the underside of his left leg. MADE IN BRIGHTON,[17] it said.

Why, he's nothing but an overlarge wind-up toy, she thought. And the very minute she thought that, she began to laugh.

And laugh.

And laugh, until she had to bend over to hold her stomach and tears leaked out of her eyes. She could feel the bubbles of laughter still rising inside, getting up her nose like sparkling soda. She could not stop herself.

"Here, now!" shouted the Beamish Boy, "no laughing! It ain't fair."

The Cheshire Cat lost his own grin. "Fight first, laughter after," he advised. "Or maybe flight first. Or fright first."

The Red Queen sneaked out of the stands and was almost off the table, clutching her crown full of money, when the Dormouse stuck out a foot.

"No going off with that moolah, Queenie," the Dormouse said, taking the crown from her and putting it on top of the teapot.

Still laughing but no longer on the edge of hysteria, Alice looked up at the Jabberwock, who had become frozen in place. Not only was he stiff, but he had turned an odd shade of gray and looked rather like a poorly built garden statue that had been out too long in the wind and rain. She leaned toward him.

"Boo!" she said, grinning.

Little cracks ran across the Jabberwock's face and down the front of his long belly.

"Double boo!" Alice said.

Another crack ran right around the Jabberwock's tail, and it broke off with a sound like a tree branch breaking.

"Triple . . ." Alice began, but stopped when someone put a hand on her arm. She turned. It was the White Queen.

"You have won, my dear," the White Queen said, placing the Red Queen's crown—minus all the money—on Alice's head. "A true queen is merciful."

Alice nodded, then thought a moment. "But where was the courage in that? All I did was laugh."

17 **Brighton:** city on the southern coast of England known for its pleasant climate and vacation areas

"Laughter in the face of certain death? It is the very definition of the Hero," said the White Queen. "The Jabberwock knew it and therefore could no longer move against you. You would have known it yourself much sooner, had that beastly Albert not been such a tattletale."

"But *I* was the tattletale," Alice said, hardly daring to breathe.

"Who do you think told Albert's sisters?" asked the White Queen. She patted a few errant strands of hair in place and simultaneously tucked several stray dollars back under her crown.

Alice digested this information for a minute, but something about the conversation was still bothering her. Then she had it. "How do *you* know about Albert?" she asked.

"I'm late!" the White Queen cried suddenly, and dashed off down the road, looking from behind like a large white rabbit.

Alice should have been surprised, but nothing ever really surprised her anymore in Wonderland.

Except . . .

except . . .

herself.

Courage, she thought.

Laughter, she thought.

Maybe I'll try them both out on Albert.

And so thinking, she felt herself suddenly rising, first slowly, then faster and faster still, up the rabbit-hole, all the way back home. ༖

ALICE WITH THE WHITE AND RED QUEENS
1865
Sir John Tenniel

Excerpt from *GREAT PLAINS*

IAN FRAZIER

Personally, I love Crazy Horse[1] because even the most basic outline of his life shows how great he was; because he remained himself from the moment of his birth to the moment he died; because he knew exactly where he wanted to live, and never left; because he may have surrendered, but he was never defeated in battle; because, although he was killed, even the Army admitted he was never captured; because he was so free that he didn't know what a jail looked like; because at the most desperate moment of his life he only cut Little Big Man[2] on the hand;

1 **Crazy Horse:** war chief of several Native American resistance bands during the 1860s to 1870s

2 **Little Big Man:** former Sioux warrior who later helped government agents; he was involved in the attempt to subdue Crazy Horse.

because, unlike many people all over the world, when he met white men he was not diminished by the encounter; because his dislike of the oncoming civilization was prophetic; because the idea of becoming a farmer apparently never crossed his mind; because he didn't end up in the Dry Tortugas;[3] because he never met the President; because he never rode on a train, slept in a boardinghouse, ate at a table; because he never wore a medal or a top hat or any other thing that white men gave him; because he made sure that his wife was safe before going to where he expected to die; because although Indian agents, among themselves, sometimes referred to Red Cloud as "Red" and Spotted Tail as "Spot," they never used a diminutive[4] for him; because, deprived of freedom, power, occupation, culture, trapped in a situation where bravery was invisible, he was still brave; because he fought in self-defense, and took no one with him when he died; because, like the rings of Saturn, the carbon atom, and the underwater reef, he belonged to a category of phenomena which our technology had not then advanced far enough to photograph; because no photograph or painting or even sketch of him exists; because he is not the Indian on the nickel, the tobacco pouch, or the apple crate. Crazy Horse was a slim man of medium height with brown hair hanging below his waist and a scar above his lip. Now, in the mind of each person who imagines him, he looks different. ❧

3 **Dry Tortugas:** small group of islands near Key West, Florida; for many years a haven for outlaws

4 **diminutive:** shortened name

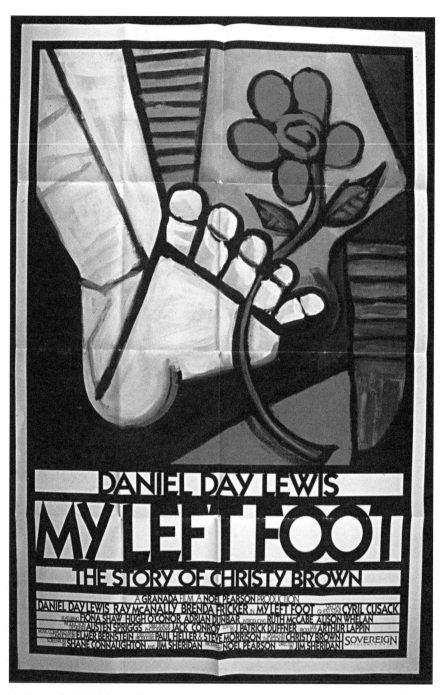

Movie poster for *My Left Foot,* 1989.

The Letter "A"

from My Left Foot

CHRISTY BROWN

I was born in the Rotunda Hospital, on June 5th, 1932. There were nine children before me and twelve after me, so I myself belong to the middle group. Out of this total of twenty-two, seventeen lived, but four died in infancy, leaving thirteen still to hold the family fort.

Mine was a difficult birth, I am told. Both mother and son almost died. A whole army of relations queued[1] up outside the hospital until the small hours of the morning, waiting for news and praying furiously that it would be good.

After my birth mother was sent to recuperate for some weeks and I was kept in the hospital while she was away. I remained there for some time, without name, for I wasn't baptized until my mother was well enough to bring me to church.

It was mother who first saw that there was something wrong with me. I was about four months old at the time. She noticed that my head had a habit of falling backward whenever she tried to feed me. She attempted to correct this by placing her hand on the back of my neck to keep it steady. But when she took it away, back it would drop again. That was the first warning sign. Then she became aware of other defects as I got older. She saw that my hands were clenched nearly all of the time and were inclined to twine behind my back, my mouth couldn't grasp the teat of the bottle because even at that early age my jaws would either lock together tightly, so that it was impossible for her to open them, or

---

1 **queued:** formed a waiting line

they would suddenly become limp and fall loose, dragging my whole mouth to one side. At six months I could not sit up without having a mountain of pillows around me. At twelve months it was the same.

Very worried by this, mother told my father her fears, and they decided to seek medical advice without any further delay. I was a little over a year old when they began to take me to hospitals and clinics, convinced that there was something definitely wrong with me, something which they could not understand or name, but which was very real and disturbing.

Almost every doctor who saw and examined me, labeled me a very interesting but also a hopeless case. Many told mother very gently that I was mentally defective and would remain so. That was a hard blow to a young mother who had already reared five healthy children. The doctors were so very sure of themselves that mother's faith in me seemed almost an impertinence.[2] They assured her that nothing could be done for me.

She refused to accept this truth, the inevitable truth—as it then seemed—that I was beyond cure, beyond saving, even beyond hope. She could not and would not believe that I was an imbecile,[3] as the doctors told her. She had nothing in the world to go by, not a scrap of evidence to support her conviction that, though my body was crippled, my mind was not. In spite of all the doctors and specialists told her, she would not agree. I don't believe she knew why—she just knew, without feeling the smallest shade of doubt.

Finding that the doctors could not help in any way beyond telling her not to place her trust in me, or, in other words, to forget I was a human creature, rather to regard me as just something to be fed and washed and then put away again, mother decided there and then to take matters into her own hands. I was *her* child, and therefore part of the family. No matter how dull and incapable I might grow up to be, she was determined to treat me on the same plane as the others, and not as the "queer one" in the back room who was never spoken of when there were visitors present.

That was a momentous decision as far as my future life was concerned. It meant that I would always have my mother on my side to help me fight all the battles that were to come, and to inspire me with new strength when I was almost beaten. But it wasn't easy for her because now the relatives and friends had decided otherwise. They contended that I should be taken kindly, sympathetically, but not seriously. That

2 **impertinence:** insult

3 **imbecile:** term once used to define persons with mental disabilities

would be a mistake. "For your own sake," they told her, "don't look to this boy as you would to the others; it would only break your heart in the end." Luckily for me, mother and father held out against the lot of them. But mother wasn't content just to say that I was not an idiot: she set out to prove it, not because of any rigid sense of duty, but out of love. That is why she was so successful.

At this time she had the five other children to look after besides the "difficult one," though as yet it was not by any means a full house. They were my brothers, Jim, Tony, and Paddy, and my two sisters, Lily and Mona, all of them very young, just a year or so between each of them, so that they were almost exactly like steps of stairs.

Four years rolled by and I was now five, and still as helpless as a newly born baby. While my father was out at bricklaying, earning our bread and butter for us, mother was slowly, patiently pulling down the wall, brick by brick, that seemed to thrust itself between me and the other children, slowly, patiently penetrating beyond the thick curtain that hung over my mind, separating it from theirs. It was hard, heartbreaking work, for often all she got from me in return was a vague smile and perhaps a faint gurgle. I could not speak or even mumble, nor could I sit up without support on my own, let alone take steps. But I wasn't inert[4] or motionless. I seemed, indeed, to be convulsed with movement, wild, stiff, snakelike movement that never left me, except in sleep. My fingers twisted and twitched continually, my arms twined backwards and would often shoot out suddenly this way and that, and my head lolled and sagged sideways. I was a queer, crooked little fellow.

Mother tells me how one day she had been sitting with me for hours in an upstairs room, showing me pictures out of a great big storybook that I had got from Santa Claus last Christmas and telling me the names of the different animals and flowers that were in them, trying without success to get me to repeat them. This had gone on for hours while she talked and laughed with me. Then at the end of it she leaned over me and said gently into my ear:

"Did you like it, Chris? Did you like the bears and the monkeys and all the lovely flowers? Nod your head for yes, like a good boy."

But I could make no sign that I had understood her. Her face was bent over mine hopefully. Suddenly, involuntarily, my queer hand reached up and grasped one of the dark curls that fell in a thick cluster about her

---

4 **inert:** lacking the power to move; inactive

neck. Gently she loosened the clenched fingers, though some dark strands were still clutched between them.

Then she turned away from my curious stare and left the room, crying. The door closed behind her. It all seemed hopeless. It looked as though there was some justification[5] for my relatives' contention that I was an idiot and beyond help.

They now spoke of an institution.

"Never!" said my mother almost fiercely, when this was suggested to her. "I know my boy is not an idiot, it is his body that is shattered, not his mind. I'm sure of that."

Sure? Yet inwardly, she prayed God would give her some proof of her faith. She knew it was one thing to believe but quite another thing to prove.

I was now five, and still I showed no real sign of intelligence. I showed no apparent interest in things except with my toes—more especially those of my left foot. Although my natural habits were clean, I could not aid myself, but in this respect my father took care of me. I used to lie on my back all the time in the kitchen, or, on bright warm days, out in the garden, a little bundle of crooked muscles and twisted nerves, surrounded by a family that loved me and hoped for me and that made me part of their own warmth and humanity. I was lonely, imprisoned in a world of my own, unable to communicate with others, cut off, separated from them as though a glass wall stood between my existence and theirs, thrusting me beyond the sphere of their lives and activities. I longed to run about and play with the rest, but I was unable to break loose from my bondage.

Then, suddenly, it happened! in a moment everything was changed, my future life molded into a definite shape, my mother's faith in me rewarded and her secret fear changed into open triumph.

It happened so quickly, so simply after all the years of waiting and uncertainty, that I can see and feel the whole scene as if it had happened last week. It was the afternoon of a cold, gray December day. The streets outside glistened with snow, the white sparkling flakes stuck and melted on the windowpanes and hung on the boughs of the trees like molten silver. The wind howled dismally, whipping up little whirling columns of snow that rose and fell at every fresh gust. And over all, the dull, murky sky stretched like a dark canopy,[6] a vast infinity of grayness.

Inside, all the family were gathered round the big kitchen fire that lit

5 **justification:** reason

6 **canopy:** a protective covering

up the little room with a warm glow and made giant shadows dance on the walls and ceiling.

In a corner Mona and Paddy were sitting, huddled together, a few torn school primers[7] before them. They were writing down little sums on to an old chipped slate,[8] using a bright piece of yellow chalk. I was close to them, propped up by a few pillows against the wall, watching.

It was the chalk that attracted me so much. It was a long, slender stick of vivid yellow. I had never seen anything like it before, and it showed up so well against the black surface of the slate that I was fascinated by it as much as if it had been a stick of gold.

Suddenly, I wanted desperately to do what my sister was doing. Then—without thinking or knowing exactly what I was doing, I reached out and took the stick of chalk out of my sister's hand—with my left foot.

I do not know why I used my left foot to do this. It is a puzzle to many people as well as to myself, for, although I had displayed a curious interest in my toes at an early age, I had never attempted before this to use either of my feet in any way. They could have been as useless to me as were my hands. That day, however, my left foot, apparently by its own volition, reached out and very impolitely took the chalk out of my sister's hand.

I held it tightly between my toes, and, acting on an impulse, made a wild sort of scribble with it on the slate. Next moment I stopped, a bit dazed, surprised, looking down at the stick of yellow chalk stuck between my toes, not knowing what to do with it next, hardly knowing how it got there. Then I looked up and became aware that everyone had stopped talking and was staring at me silently. Nobody stirred. Mona, her black curls framing her chubby little face, stared at me with great big eyes and open mouth. Across the open hearth, his face lit by flames, sat my father, leaning forward, hands outspread on his knees, his shoulders tense. I felt the sweat break out on my forehead.

My mother came in from the pantry with a steaming pot in her hand. She stopped midway between the table and the fire, feeling the tension flowing through the room. She followed their stare and saw me in the corner. Her eyes looked from my face down to my foot, with the chalk gripped between my toes. She put down the pot.

Then she crossed over to me and knelt down beside me, as she had done so many times before.

---

7 **primers:** textbooks used for teaching introductory subjects
8 **slate:** a hand-held chalkboard

"I'll show you what to do with it, Chris," she said, very slowly and in a queer, choked way, her face flushed as if with some inner excitement.

Taking another piece of chalk from Mona, she hesitated, then very deliberately drew, on the floor in front of me, *the single letter "A."*

"Copy that," she said, looking steadily at me. "Copy it, Christy."

I couldn't.

I looked about me, looked around at the faces that were turned towards me, tense, excited faces that were at that moment frozen, immobile, eager, waiting for a miracle in their midst.

The stillness was profound. The room was full of flame and shadow that danced before my eyes and lulled my taut nerves into a sort of waking sleep. I could hear the sound of the water tap dripping in the pantry, the loud ticking of the clock on the mantelshelf, and the soft hiss and crackle of the logs on the open hearth.

I tried again. I put out my foot and made a wild jerking stab with the chalk which produced a very crooked line and nothing more. Mother held the slate steady for me.

"Try again, Chris," she whispered in my ear. "Again."

I did. I stiffened my body and put my left foot out again, for the third time. I drew one side of the letter. I drew half the other side. Then the stick of chalk broke and I was left with a stump. I wanted to fling it away and give up. Then I felt my mother's hand on my shoulder. I tried once more. Out went my foot. I shook, I sweated and strained every muscle. My hands were so tightly clenched that my fingernails bit into the flesh. I set my teeth so hard that I nearly pierced my lower lip. Everything in the room swam till the faces around me were mere patches of white. But—I drew it—*the letter "A."* There it was on the floor before me. Shaky, with awkward, wobbly sides and a very uneven center line. But it *was* the letter "A." I looked up. I saw my mother's face for a moment, tears on her cheeks. Then my father stooped and hoisted me on to his shoulder.

I had done it! It had started—the thing that was to give my mind its chance of expressing itself. True, I couldn't speak with my lips. But now I would speak through something more lasting than spoken words—written words.

That one letter, scrawled on the floor with a broken bit of yellow chalk gripped between my toes, was my road to a new world, my key to mental freedom. It was to provide a source of relaxation to the tense, taut thing that was I, which panted for expression behind a twisted mouth. ∾

Those Winter Sundays

ROBERT HAYDEN

Sundays too my father got up early
and put his clothes on in the blueblack cold,
then with cracked hands that ached
from labor in the weekday weather made
banked fires blaze. No one ever thanked him.

I'd wake and hear the cold splintering, breaking.
When the rooms were warm, he'd call,
and slowly I would rise and dress,
fearing the chronic angers of that house,

Speaking indifferently to him,
who had driven out the cold
and polished my good shoes as well.
What did I know, what did I know
of love's austere and lonely offices?

Sir Bors Fights for a Lady

ROSEMARY SUTCLIFF

For three days after parting from his companions of the Round Table,[1] Sir Bors rode through the forest ways alone. And at evening on the third day he came to a tall, strong-built tower rising dark against the sunset, in the midst of a clearing. He beat upon the deep arched gate, to ask for a night's lodging, and was welcomed in. His horse was led to the stables and himself up to the Great Chamber high in the tower, full of honey-golden sunset light from its western windows that looked away over the treetops. There he was greeted by the lady of the place, who was fair and sweet to look upon, but poorly clad in a patched gown of faded leaf-green silk.

She bade him to sit by her at supper; and when the food was brought in, he saw that it was as poor as her gown, and was sorry for her sake, though for his own it made little difference, for he had taken a vow at the outset, that he would eat no meat and drink no wine while he followed the Quest of the Holy Grail;[2] and so he touched nothing but the bread set before his place, and asked one of the table squires for a cup of water. And seeing this, the lady said, "Ah, sir knight, I know well that the food is poor and rough, but do not disdain it, it is the best we have."

"Lady, forgive me," said Bors, and flushed to the roots of his russet[3] hair, "it is because your food is too good and your wine too rich that I eat bread and drink water, for I have vowed to touch nothing else, while I am

---

1 **Round Table:** medieval court of King Arthur and his knights
2 **Quest of the Holy Grail:** journey in search of the cup used by Christ at the Last Supper. Some attributed supernatural powers to this holy relic.
3 **russet:** reddish brown

GOD SPEED
1900
Edmund Blair-Leighton

on the quest that I follow."

"And what quest is that?"

"The Quest of the Holy Grail."

"I have heard of this quest, and I know you, therefore, for one of King Arthur's knights, the greatest champions in the world," said the lady; and it seemed as though she might have said more, but at that moment a squire came hurrying into the room.

"Madam, it goes ill with us—your sister has taken two more of your castles, and sends you word that she will leave you not one square foot of land, if by tomorrow's noon you have not found a knight to fight for you against her lord!"

Then the lady pressed her hands over her face and wept, until Sir Bors said to her, "Pray you, lady, tell me the meaning of this."

"I will tell you," said the lady. "The lord of these parts once loved my elder sister, never knowing what like she was—what like she is—and by little and little, while they were together, he gave over to her all his power, so that in truth she became the ruler. And her rule was a harsh one, causing the death and maiming and imprisonment of many of his people. Learning wisdom on his deathbed, and listening at last to the distress of his folk, he drove her out and made me his successor in her place, that I might undo what could be undone of the harm. But no sooner was he dead than my sister took a new lord, Priadan the Black, and made alliance with him to wage war on me." She spread her hands. "Good sir, the rest you must know."

"Who and what is this Priadan the Black?" said Bors.

"The greatest champion and the cruellest and most dreaded tyrant in these parts."

"Then send word to your sister, that you have found a knight to fight for you at tomorrow's noon."

Then the lady wept again, for joy. "God give you strength tomorrow," she said, "for it is surely by his sending that you are come here today!"

Next morning, Sir Bors heard Mass in the chapel of the tower, and then went out to the courtyard, where the lady had summoned all the knights yet remaining to her, that they might witness the coming conflict. She would have had him eat before he armed, but he refused, saying that he would fight fasting, and eat after he had fought; and so the squires helped him to buckle on his harness; and he mounted and rode out through the gate, the lady riding a grey palfrey[4] at his side to guide

---

| 4 **palfrey:** a tame, slow-trotting horse

him to the meeting place, and all her people, even to the castle scullions,[5] following after.

They had not ridden far when they came to a level meadow at the head of a valley, and saw a great crowd of people waiting for them, with a fine striped pavilion pitched in their midst. And as they rode out from the long morning shadows of the trees, out from the shadow of the pavilion appeared a damsel in a gown of rose-scarlet damask[6] mounted on a fine bay mare.

"That is my sister," said the lady, "and beside her, look, Priadan, her lord and champion."

The sisters pricked forward to meet each other in the centre of the meadow; and beside the damsel of the pavilion rode a huge knight in armour as black as his tall warhorse; and beside the lady of the tower rode Sir Bors, feeling the balance of his lance.[7]

"Sister," said Sir Bors's lady, "as I sent you word last evening, I have found a champion to fight for my rights, in the matter between us."

"*Rights*!" cried the elder sister. "You played upon my lord when he was in his dotage,[8] until you had wheedled out of him what is truly mine. These are your *rights*!"

"Damsel," said Sir Bors, "your sister has told me the other side of that story. It is she whom I believe, and it is she whom I will fight for this day."

And the two champions looked at each other, each searching out the eye-flicker behind the dark slits of his opponent's helmet.

"Let us waste no more time in talking," said Priadan the Black, "for it was not to talk that we came here."

So the onlookers fell back, leaving a clear space down the midst of the meadow, and the two champions drew apart to opposite ends of it, then wheeled their horses and with levelled lances spurred towards each other. Faster and faster, from canter to full gallop, the spur clods flying from beneath their hooves, until at last they clashed together like two stags battling for the lordship of the herd. Both lances ran true to target, and splintered into kindling wood, and both knights were swept backward over their horses' cruppers[9] to the ground.

---

5 **scullions:** kitchen helpers

6 **damask:** a heavy, lustrous, patterned fabric

7 **lance:** long steel-tipped spear carried by knights

8 **dotage:** state of senile decay; old age

9 **cruppers:** leather loops which pass under a horse's tail and buckle to the saddle

With the roar of the crowd like a stormy sea in his ears, Sir Bors was up again on the instant, the Black Knight also. And drawing their swords they fell upon each other with such mighty blows that their shields were soon hacked to rags of painted wood, and the sparks flew from their blades as they rang together and slashed through the mail[10] on flanks and shoulders to set the red blood running. They were so evenly matched that it came to Bors that he must use his head as well as his sword arm, if he was going to carry off the victory. And he began to fight on the defensive, saving his strength and letting his opponent use up his own powers in pressing on to make an end.

The crowd yelled, and the lady he fought for hid her face in her hands. And Sir Bors gave ground a little, and then gave ground again, Priadan pressing after him, until at last he felt the Black Knight beginning to tire, his feet becoming slower, his sword strokes less sure. Then, as though fresh life was suddenly flowing into him, Bors began to press forward in his turn, raining his blows upon the other man, beating him this way and that, until Sir Priadan stumbled like a drunk man, and in the end went over backwards on the trampled turf.

Then Sir Bors bestrode[11] him, and dragged off his helmet and flung it aside, and upswung his sword as though he would have struck Sir Priadan's head from his shoulders and flung it after his helmet.

When Sir Priadan saw the bright arc of the blade above him, he seemed to grow small and grovelling[12] inside his champion's armour, and cried out shrilly, "Quarter![13] You cannot kill me, I am crying quarter!" and then as Sir Bors still stood over him with menacing sword, "Oh, for God's sweet sake have mercy on me and let me live! I will swear never again to wage war on the lady you serve! I will promise anything you ask, if only you will let me live!"

And Sir Bors lowered his blade, feeling sick, and said, "Remember that oath. And now get out of my sight!'

And the Black Knight scrambled to his feet and made off, running low like a beaten cur.[14]

And the elder sister gave a shrill, furious cry, and set her horse at the onlookers who jostled back to let her by; and so dashed through them

10 **mail:** armor made of finely-woven metal links
11 **bestrode:** stood over with feet firmly planted on either side
12 **grovelling:** submissive
13 **Quarter:** a plea for mercy
14 **cur:** a mongrel; dog

and away, rowelling[15] her mare's flanks until the blood on them ran bright as her rose-scarlet gown.

When all those who had come with her and Sir Priadan her lord saw what manner of champion they had followed, they came and swore allegiance to the lady of the tower. And so, with great rejoicing, she and her household rode back the way they had come. And in the Great Chamber of the tower, Sir Bors sat down and ate and drank at last, though still only bread and water; and the lady herself bathed and salved[16] his wounds.

And after he had rested for a day or so, he set out once more on his quest. ❧

15: **rowelling:** spurring; kicking with spurs

16 **salved:** applied a soothing remedy

Elizabeth Blackwell: Medical Pioneer

JOANNA HALPERT KRAUS

PERCUSSION PLAYER *flips sign on easel to read "Philadelphia."* ELIZA-BETH BLACKWELL *appears, attired in a modest gown and bonnet, carrying a small travelling case. She is in her mid-20s stubborn, determined, restless, and independent. She mimes walking in place.*

The NARRATORS *take poses backs to us in separate parts of the stage.*

ELIZABETH *flings her arms wide to the world, as she sets her case down.*

ELIZABETH. I want to be —

NARRATOR ONE (*turns*). Want to be—

NARRATOR TWO (*turns*). Want to be —

ELIZABETH. The first lady surgeon in the United States. No. I want to be the first—in the entire world!

NARRATOR ONE. The first—

NARRATOR TWO. In the world.

NARRATOR THREE (*turns*). CRAZY! (NARRATORS *confer.*)

NARRATOR ONE. Not practical.

NARRATOR TWO (*authoritatively*). A well brought up lady cannot be a doctor.

NARRATOR ONE (*reading from a large period magazine*). "A woman's sphere is in the home." (*Closes magazine decisively.*)

NARRATOR THREE (*reading from a book*). *The Young Lady's Book* says she must be "obedient, submissive and humble."

NARRATORS *look at one another, then back at* ELIZABETH, *glaring at her.*

NARRATOR ONE. Shocking!

NARRATOR TWO. Shameful!

NARRATOR THREE. Sinful!

ALL NARRATORS (*pointing at* ELIZABETH). SCANDALOUS!

NARRATORS *exit.* DR. BARNES *enters. 40s. Wise, pragmatic.*

DR. BARNES. My dear Miss Blackwell, woman was designed to be the helpmate of man. Man must be the physician; woman the nurse.

ELIZABETH. Doctor, I've paid for three years of pre-medical study with you. I've attended your lectures, used your library, been with you to visit patients. Please! You've got to help me get admitted to medical school.

DR. BARNES. No woman has ever gone to medical school!

ELIZABETH. You told me I had the ability.

DR. BARNES. You do! But it's 1847, Miss Blackwell. There isn't a college in the country that will accept you.

ELIZABETH. Times won't change unless we make them change!

DR. BARNES (*slowly*). There is one way.

ELIZABETH. What? What?

DR. BARNES. Disguise yourself as a man, and go study in Paris.

ELIZABETH (*shocked*). How can I help other women, if I'm in disguise? There must be some school, one school, in this huge nation brave enough to accept a woman. Won't you please write a letter on my behalf?

DR. BARNES. I'll do better than that! I'll send you to a friend, who's Dean of Admissions here in Philadelphia. But don't expect miracles.

ELIZABETH. Miracles are something you make happen!

DR. BARNES *exits,* ELIZABETH *crosses to a new level, and* DEAN REYNOLDS *enters. He is in his 40s, imperious and patronizing.*

DEAN REYNOLDS. I've agreed to see you as a courtesy to my colleague, Miss Blackwell. What is it you want?

ELIZABETH. I want to go to medical school.

DEAN REYNOLDS. You can't be serious.

ELIZABETH. I've never been more serious in my life.

DEAN REYNOLDS. Then you're a lunatic.

ELIZABETH. Why won't you consider my request?

DEAN REYNOLDS. Miss Blackwell, it's not seemly or suitable for a lady. (*Peers over his glasses.*) I presume you are one, to pursue such a calling. Why you'd faint at the first dissection, you'd flinch at the first sign of blood. You'd disrupt the entire class.

ELIZABETH. I've done dissections as part of my pre-medical studies.

DEAN REYNOLDS. An unfortunate mistake on my colleague's part.

DEAN REYNOLDS *exits.* SOUND: *door slams shut.*

ELIZABETH (*to closed door*). And I never flinched or fainted. (*To herself.*) Well, just the first time. He wouldn't even listen to me!

ELIZABETH *marches back to her room and takes out a writing box and begins a letter.*

Dear Sir, I wish to apply to your medical college.

As she writes, DEAN SNYDER, JAMES *and* ARTHUR *enter a different area.* DEAN SNYDER *is 40s, hard-nosed.* JAMES *is his colleague, 30s. A "yes" person.*

DEAN SNYDER (*waving Elizabeth's letter*). If we admit a woman, our enrollment will decline. Therefore, I urge us all to reject the application, despite a fine recommendation.

JAMES (*appplauding*). Hear! Hear!

DEAN SNYDER. She can hardly expect us to give her a stick with which to break our own heads! (*To James*) Do you know what will happen if women patients start going to women doctors?

JAMES. What?

DEAN REYNOLDS. We'll lose our jobs! This is the most absurd application I've ever had. Suddenly there are all these quacks trying to get into medical college. With water cures, electrical cures. We might as well let in all the charlatans[1] as let in a woman!

They exit. ELIZABETH *opens her letter, reading.*

ELIZABETH. Rejection from Philadelphia. (*Throws it down. Opens another letter.* NARRATORS *have entered.*) Rejection from New York.

ELIZABETH *crosses to* DR. BARNES' *parlor, who enters as the rejections increase.*

NARRATOR ONE. Three.

NARRATOR TWO. Six.

NARRATOR THREE. Twelve.

DR. BARNES. Elizabeth, don't give up yet. If the big fish won't let you swim, try the little fish.

ELIZABETH. Do you think it'll make any difference?

DR. BARNES. It might. All you can do is try.

ELIZABETH *returns to her room and* DR. BARNES *remains sitting and reading his medical journal, as* NARRATORS *continue.*

NARRATOR ONE. But the results were—

NARRATOR TWO. Fifteen rejects.

NARRATOR THREE. Twenty five rejections.

ELIZABETH (*thinks aloud*). All these years I've tried to earn enough to pay for medical school. Teaching music to children who are tone deaf. Trying to pound an education into students, who don't care. All these years trying to prepare for medical school, learning Greek, learning anatomy.[2] But it doesn't matter how hard I've worked. As soon as they see my name, Elizabeth, the answer is "No!" Because I'm a female. That's the only reason.

ELIZABETH *turns away from audience as staff of Geneva Medical College enters:* DEAN RICHARDS, *smooth administrator;* RAYMOND, *his first colleague, action-oriented;* HERBERT, *his second colleague, who follows the rules. all are men in their 30s.*

---

1 **charlatans:** quacks; frauds
2 **anatomy:** study of the structure of a body

PERCUSSION PLAYER *flips sign to read "Geneva, New York."*

DEAN RICHARDS. We have a very awkward situation, gentlemen. I need your advice.

RAYMOND AND HERBERT (*turn*). Y-e-e-s.

DEAN RICHARDS (*with a sheaf of papers*). A well qualified applicant. With an excellent recommendation from Dr. Barnes.

RAYMOND. Philadelphia's best! Find a scholarship for him. Any candidate he recommends, I say we take.

DEAN RICHARDS. I'm afraid it's a graver matter than mere scholarship.

RAYMOND. More serious than money?

HERBERT. An incurable disease?

DEAN RICHARDS. You might say so. The fact is, gentleman—(*Pauses.*) The **he** is a **she**.

HERBERT. A she!

SOUND: percussion.

RAYMOND. Out of the question!

HERBERT. Impossible.

DEAN RICHARDS. I agree. Of course. But what do we write Dr. Barnes?

HERBERT. We don't want to insult him.

DEAN RICHARDS. We want to keep his good will. (*They pace.*)

RAYMOND. The request is highly unusual and it concerns the students. Let them decide!

DEAN RICHARDS. Brilliant! And if any of the students object to admitting a woman, we'll reject the application.

HERBERT. The students have never agreed on anything!

DEAN RICHARDS (*smoothly*). Then we can tell Dr. Barnes it was the students' decision—not ours!

They exit, as students enter a different area. JOHN, *Student Council President, is 18; bright, fair-minded but not above pranks.* ELMER, *17, is bored. Anything for a laugh.* PHILLIP, *17, is a reactionary.*[3]

JOHN (*bangs gavel*). I call this meeting of the Student Council to order.

---

3 **reactionary:** an ultra-conservative person who opposes change

SOUND: *Hoots, whistles, catcalls.*

ELMER. Hurry it up.

PHILLIP. All members present.

JOHN. Good! The Dean has asked the Student Council to make a momentous decision. One that could change this institution.

ELMER. Anything for a change.

JOHN. A lady has applied to Geneva Medical College.

PHILLIP. Can't be a lady if she applied here.

SOUND: *Raucous laughter.*

JOHN. The Dean wants our decision this afternoon. May we have some discussion?

ELMER. Heck, just for argument's sake, I say let her come. She'd liven up the place.

PHILLIP. Liven up the place! She'd ruin our reputation!

JOHN. She could put Geneva Medical College on the map.

PHILLIP. If we let her in, she'll slow the whole class down.

ELMER (to PHILLIP). Then someone else besides you would be at the bottom!

SOUND: *Laughter.*

JOHN. It's my belief scientific education should be open to all.

PHILLIP. I agree. As long as "all" ain't women!

SOUND: *More laughter.*

ELMER. Call the vote! Call the vote!

JOHN. All those in favor?

PHILLIP. Aye!

SOUND: *Simultaneous chorus of Ayes.*

JOHN. All those opposed?

PHILLIP. NAY!

ELMER *rushes to* PHILLIP *and punches him and keeps pounding him.* PHILLIP *fights back but is no match.*

ELMER. Toss him out the window! Throw him down the stairs!

PHILLIP (*hastily*). Aye! Aye! I vote Aye!

JOHN. Then it's unanimous! (*Grinning.*) This is more fun than Halloween!

SOUND: *Yeas, whistles, catcalls as* STUDENTS *exit.* PERCUSSION PLAYER *flips sign to read "Philadelphia."* SOUND: *Knock.* BETSY, *an 8 to 10 year old servant, active, curious, mimes running up the stairs.*

BETSY (*Rushes in to Elizabeth's room*). Miss Blackwell. A letter for you.

ELIZABETH. Thank you.

BETSY. Ain't ya gonna open it? I ran up two flights. I never saw anyone get so many letters as you do, Miss Blackwell. More than the Doctor himself. You get more than anyone in the whole city of Philadelphia, I warrant.[4]

ELIZABETH. But they all say the same. They all say No.

BETSY. The Doctor and the Missus say you're to come down for tea. Hot mince pies,[5] Miss Blackwell.

ELIZABETH. In a minute. I will in a minute.

Betsy exits. LILY BARNES, *the doctor's wife, brings tea into the parlor.* LILY *is in her 30s, supportive. Unobtrusively she puts the tea out, as* ELIZABETH *opens her letter half-heartedly.* ELIZABETH *rises, more and more astonished by the letter's content. She races out of her room, delirious with joy.*

Everybody! Listen! Everybody!

ELIZABETH *flies in to the parlor and whirls around the room.*

I've been accepted.

LILY BARNES (*hugs* ELIZABETH). Congratulations.

DR. BARNES. I knew one of those schools would have common sense.

ELIZABETH. They've approved me. Gentlemen—(*Curtsies to an imaginary group.*) I accept.

LILY BARNES. When will you leave?

ELIZABETH. Immediately! Before they change their minds!

DR. BARNES *brings* ELIZABETH *her travel case and exits as* ELIZABETH *crosses to a new area and* LILY BARNES *exits with tea tray.* NARRATOR ONE *enters.*

PERCUSSION PLAYER *flips sign to read "Geneva, New York."*

NARRATOR ONE. But her troubles were just beginning

---

4 **warrant:** declare

5 **mince pies:** chopped meat pies; similar to pot pies of today

SOUND: *Door knocker.* ELIZABETH *knocks and waits.* MRS. TROTTER, *50s, landlady, tight-lipped respectability, opens the door.*

ELIZABETH. I'd like to rent a room.

MRS. TROTTER (*Suspiciously*). Traveling by yourself?

ELIZABETH. No. I've come to study at Geneva Medical College.

MRS. TROTTER. A woman doctor? I should say not! I run a respectable boarding house!

SOUND: *Door slams: Wearily,* ELIZABETH *goes to next house as* MRS. GILES, *40s, landlady, open-minded, kind, enters.* ELIZABETH *knocks.* SOUND: *A different kind of knocker or bell.* MRS. GILES *opens the door.*

ELIZABETH. Please don't say no! This is the last boarding house on my list. I've got to rent a room. Classes have already started.

MRS. GILES (*fascinated*). You're going to medical college?

ELIZABETH. Yes.

MRS. GILES (*dubious*). Never heard of no woman doctor before. Can you cure headaches? I get powerful headaches.

ELIZABETH. I'll try. (MRS. GILES *appraises her.*)

MRS. GILES (*slowly*). Maybe I could let you have the room up in the attic. (*Warns*) Not much heat!

ELIZABETH. I'll take it.

MRS. GILES. You look like a proper young lady. Not in any trouble are you?

ELIZABETH *puts her bag in the doorway.*

ELIZABETH (*offers money*). I'll pay six weeks in advance.

MRS. GILES *hesitates, then accepts it.*

MRS. GILES. Now mind, don't expect other folks to talk to you at dinner. Never heard of no lady doctor!

MRS. GILES *ushers* ELIZABETH *off.*

SOUND: *Graduation procession march.*

DR. BENJAMIN HALE, *Geneva Medical College president, enters. 40s, dignified, He wears a black velvet mortarboard to suggest academic regalia.*[6]

---

6 **mortarboard . . . regalia:** an academic cap with flat, square top; usually worn at graduations to indicate educational achievement

DR. HALE (*addresses audience*). No one at the college expected her to show up. And when she did no one thought she'd stay. And certainly no one ever thought she'd graduate with top honors!

SOUND: Applause, Processional march as ELIZABETH *comes forward.*

Dr. Blackwell! Congratulations! (*Hands her diploma.*)

ELIZABETH. Dr. Benjamin Hale, faculty, family, friends, ladies and gentlemen, I will do everything in my power to bring honor to this diploma. I promise you!

SOUND: More wild applause. Shouts of "Hurrah for Elizabeth." DR. BENJAMIN HALE *exits as* NARRATORS *enter and* ELIZABETH *crosses to a new area.*

NARRATOR ONE. Elizabeth tried to keep her promise.

NARRATOR TWO. She went to Paris to fulfill her dream.

NARRATOR THREE. But no hospital would admit her.

ELIZABETH. What good is my diploma!

NARRATOR TWO. Only the maternity hospital would take her. As a—

ELIZABETH (*reading the letter, shocked*). Student nurse. A STUDENT NURSE! I have a medical degree! (*Squares her shoulder, determined.*) If that's how I have to start, then I will! (*Reflects.*) Besides, I'll learn more in three months there, than in three years reading books.

ELIZABETH *picks up her traveling bag and marches over to don a hospital apron of heavy toweling with huge pockets.*

SOUND: PERCUSSION PLAYERS *beat a fast rhythm under chanted work poem.* ELIZABETH *mimes portion of the work poem.*

NARRATOR THREE. Work.

NARRATOR ONE. Up at five.

NARRATOR TWO. Scrub the floors.

Elizabeth Blackwell's diploma, Geneva Medical College, 1849.

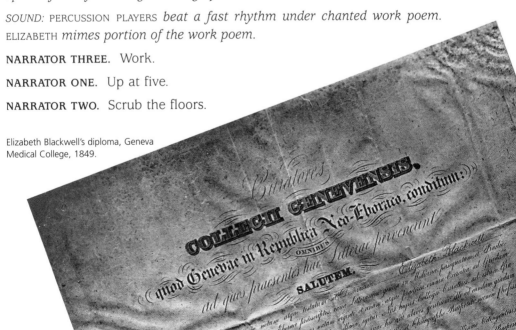

NARRATOR THREE. Dust the corners. Fill the pans.

NARRATOR ONE. Feed the patients.

NARRATOR TWO. Class at seven.

NARRATOR THREE. Follow doctors.

NARRATOR ONE. Visit wards.

NARRATOR TWO. Rushing, rushing.

NARRATOR THREE. Bolt it down.

NARRATOR ONE. A bit of bread.

NARRATOR TWO. A chunk of cheese.

NARRATOR THREE. On the run. On the run.

NARRATOR ONE. Babies born. Night and day.

NARRATOR TWO. Day and night.

NARRATOR THREE. Complications.

NARRATOR ONE. Operations.

NARRATOR TWO. Emergencies. Emergencies.

NARRATOR THREE. Middle of the night.

NARRATOR ONE. Middle of the day.

NARRATOR TWO. No sleep.

NARRATOR THREE. No time.

NARRATOR ONE. No sleep.

NARRATOR TWO. Night after night.

NARRATOR THREE. Day after day.

NARRATOR ONE. Day and night.

NARRATOR TWO. Night and day.

NARRATOR THREE. Work!

ELIZABETH *collapses in a chair and falls asleep.* NARRATORS *exit.*

SOUND: *Church bells chime three.*

LULU *runs on and shakes* ELIZABETH. LULU *is a new student nurse. 20s. Anxious.*

LULU. Mademoiselle! Mademoiselle Blackwell!

ELIZABETH (*groggy*). So tired. Go away, please. So tired.

LULU. The baby's worse.

ELIZABETH (*jumps up*). I'll be right there.

ELIZABETH *runs down the hall to the ward. She picks up the swaddled baby.* LULU *hovers in the background.*

SOUND: Baby crying.

(*Soothing.*) Sh-h. Of course, it hurts. You can't see. Not with that infection in your eyes.

ELIZABETH *puts baby back in the crib.*

Sh-h. There now. Lie still. I have to use the syringe. Lie still. If only the light were better.

SOUND: Sharp, discordant.

ELIZABETH *screams.*

OH-H-H-H! OW-W-W-W-W! OH-H-H-H

LULU *runs off.*

SOUND: More discordant sounds to indicate the passage of time.

DR. CLAUDE BLOT *enters a different area. Mid-20s. He is an intern at La Maternité. Knowledgeable.*

ELIZABETH *covers her left eye with her hand and crosses to* DR. BLOT.

DR. BLOT (*very concerned.*). How did it happen, Mademoiselle?

ELIZABETH. I was syringing the fluid from the baby's eye. I was very tired; the light was bad. Somehow when I leaned over the crib, some of the fluid squirted into my eye. (*Attempting to make light of it.*) You know the way a lemon squirts.

DR. BLOT (*examining*). More serious than a lemon, Mademoiselle. Why didn't you come to me as soon as it happened?

ELIZABETH. I had so much to do. I washed the eye out immediately. But this morning I couldn't open it at all.

DR. BLOT (*still examining*). The left eye is very inflamed and swollen. I pray to God it doesn't spread.

ELIZABETH. How am I going to work in the wards today?

DR. BLOT. You're not. Not for quite some time, Mademoiselle.

ELIZABETH (*shocked*). Not work!

DR. BLOT (*gently but firmly*). That's an order.

ELIZABETH. But I have to!

DR. BLOT. What you have to do, Mademoiselle, is get well. Unfortunately, you have the same disease as the baby you were treating.

ELIZABETH. The same? Are you sure?

DR. BLOT. It's a classic case of punilent ophthalmia.[7] I'm sure you know the dangers already.

ELIZABETH (*slowly*). With a baby, it can mean permanent blindness. That's why I was trying so hard to save his sight.

DR. BLOT. You're a doctor, so I'll be frank. There's no guarantee—

ELIZABETH (*distraught*). Doctor, can you save my eye? Can you?

DR. BLOT. I will do everything I can. But I'm a doctor, not a magician.

SOUND: *To indicate the passage of time. Narrators help Elizabeth remove hospital apron.* DR. BLOT *bends over* ELIZABETH *with a pincer.*

Are you ready? I'm going to remove the film from the pupil of your eye.

He performs the delicate procedure.

Sit up very slowly, You've been in bed for three weeks.

ELIZABETH *does.*

Now tell me what you can see.

ELIZABETH (*as she looks*). Pull the curtains and I will.

DR. BLOT (*stunned*). Mademoiselle. . . there are no curtains.

ELIZABETH (*grabbing and holding* DR. BLOT's *hand.*). Doctor, tell me I'll get better! Please tell me I'll get better. A surgeon cannot be blind!

DR. BLOT. Mademoiselle, you mustn't excite yourself. Your sister's here. She's come to take you home.

ELIZABETH. Doctor, tell me the truth, please. Am I blind?

DR. BLOT (*upset*). We used the latest medical procedures. And I was there. Every day. Every night.

ELIZABETH (*quietly*). Will I see again?

---

7 **punilent ophthalmia**: scientific name for a contagious eye disease

DR. BLOT. You might regain the sight in your right eye. But only if you have absolute rest. That's why I've sent for your sister.

ELIZABETH. And the left eye?

DR. BLOT (*shakes his head*). I did all I could. I wish to God, I could have done more.

ANNA *rushes in. 30. She is* ELIZABETH'S *older sister. Protective.* DR. BLOT *exits.*

ANNA. Elizabeth!

ELIZABETH. Anna! Anna! (ELIZABETH *starts to cry.*)

ANNA. Don't, Elizabeth. Don't.

ELIZABETH. Anna, I can't give up. For years I've planned. For years!

ANNA *holds her as* ELIZABETH *sobs silently.*

ANNA. We can't always do what we planned. Now, you must get your strength back.

ELIZABETH. What's the point in getting well, Anna, unless I can follow my dream?

ANNA. Sh-h. Put this shawl around you. It's cold outside.

ANNA *helps* ELIZABETH *cross to a chair in a different area.*

SOUND: *To indicate the passage of time.*

ELIZABETH (*calls*). Anna! Anna!

ANNA (*rushed in*). What is it? What's wrong, Elizabeth?

ELIZABETH. I can see the lamp. On the table. It's like through a mist. But I can see it. I can see it.

ANNA *hugs her.*

ANNA. I've waited six months to hear you say that! Oh, Elizabeth. Finally. Your eyes are beginning to heal! (*Producing a letter.*) A letter came this afternoon from St. Bartholomew's Hospital in London.

ELIZABETH. Read it! Don't keep me in suspense. Quick! Is it yes or no?

ANNA *quickly hopes before she opens the letter to read it.*

ANNA. It's. . .YES! For next fall. You've been accepted to study surgery. Or to study practical medicine.

ELIZABETH. SURGERY! They accepted me! Anna, cover my eyes. Quickly! One at a time. First the left.

ANNA *covers the left eye.*

ANNA. What do you see?

ELIZABETH. You. Better than before. You're wearing a yellow dress.

ANNA *smiles.* ELIZABETH *looks hungrily.*

> And the brass lamp. The mist is lifting. And the flowered wallpaper. And tomorrow I'll see even more. The right eye is healing. It's healing! I'm sure of it! (*Tensely.*) Now cover it.

ANNA *covers the right eye.*

ANNA (*anxiously*). Can you see anything?

There is a horrible pause.

ELIZABETH. Darkness. A wall. (*With a sob.*) Anna, Anna, how do you give up a dream!

ANNA (*gently*). By dreaming another.

ANNA *holds her distraught sister in her arms. Abruptly* ELIZABETH *holds her head up. She's made a decision.*

ELIZABETH. Write St. Bartholomew's Hospital. I'm coming.

ANNA. Coming?

ELIZABETH. Not surgery. That door is closed. Forever. But dear sister, Anna, didn't you just say "dream another."

ANNA. But I meant—

ELIZABETH. Practical medicine! Tell them I'll study that. If I can't be a surgeon, Anna, I will be a doctor!

ELIZABETH *crosses to new area, as* ANNA *exits and* NARRATORS *enter.*

PERCUSSION PLAYER *flips sign to read "New York City."*

As NARRATORS *speak, two crowd members,* ANTHONY *and* HELGA, *enter.* ANTHONY, *20s, is a recent immigrant, angry.* HELGA, *also 20s and a recent immigrant, is curious.*

NARRATOR ONE. After St. Bartholomew's Elizabeth returned to America ready to be a doctor.

NARRATOR TWO. But it was a constant struggle.

NARRATOR THREE. No hospital wanted to hire her.

NARRATOR ONE. No landlord wanted to rent space to her.

NARRATOR TWO. Finally she opened a clinic in the immigrant slums of New York City.

NARRATOR THREE. Her medical ideas were shocking!

ELIZABETH *stands on a platform addressing a crowd.*

ELIZABETH. Fresh air, exercise, a balanced diet. Children are born to live, not die!

ANTHONY. We need a doctor, who can cure the cholera![8] Not a preacher!

HELGA. What's fresh air got to do with tuberculosis?[9]

ELIZABETH. Everything! Everything! If the body can't breathe, if the body isn't clean, if the body is malnourished, it cannot get well!

SOUND: Applause and boos.

NARRATOR ONE. She worked round the clock seeing patients, sometimes the only figure on a darkened street hurrying though the night to save someone.

ZAC *enters, crosses to clinic area.* ZAC, *20s, a physician, is* ELIZABETH'S *colleague.*

NARRATOR TWO. But one tragic night, a few months later, a patient died.

SOUND: Angry voices, threatening mob.

PERCUSSION PLAYERS *add to the noise of the crowd. If possible, they become crowd members.*

ANTHONY *runs across stage, yelling toward the hospital area.*

ANTHONY. Call yourself a doctor, do you? You killed her. My sister. The lady doctor killed her. And I've got a good mind to do the same to you. Murderer!

SOUND: Approaching footsteps, voices screaming.

From the hospital area, ELIZABETH *and* ZAC *peer nervously out a hospital window.*

ELIZABETH. I'd better stop that mob before they break in.

ZAC *holds* ELIZABETH *back.*

ZAC. Elizabeth, they've got pickaxes and shovels. And rocks. If you walk out there, you'll start a riot!

SOUND: Window glass shattering.

---

8 **cholera:** a violent stomach and intestinal ailment, often deadly

9 **tuberculosis:** communicable disease affecting the lungs

ELIZABETH (*shakes loose*). The riot's already started! Someone has to stop it.

SEAN, *late 20s, a burly Irish longshoreman, races on and bounds up a higher platform area carrying a huge stick.*

ZAC (*looks out*). Wait. There's a man bounding up the stairs.

They peer out.

SOUND: *Crowd noises.*

SEAN. Quiet! Quiet down, all of you. One more rock, and I'll get the entire New York police force here. (*Grins.*) And five of them are my own brothers.

SOUND: *Laughter.* SEAN *holds out his stick.*

Anybody who tries to hurt the good doctor will have to get past me first! Now, listen!

SOUND: *Noise subsides.*

Dr. Blackwell saved my wife, when she nearly died of pneumonia. How many of you out there have husbands, wives and children she's tended?

SOUND: *Crowd mumbles.*

I thought so. And did she come to your home, when you were too sick to go out?

SOUND: *Crowd mumbles in agreement. "Aye." "Yes, she did," etc.*

Did you get the same care, whether you paid or not?

SOUND: *Crowd louder in agreement. "Yes." "We did." "That's true," etc.*

Some of you couldn't stand here and screech your lungs out, if she hadn't given you the strength!

SOUND: *Crowd ad-libs. "She saved my boy." "You're right," etc.*

Are you forgetting that even a doctor can't keep a patient from dying, when it's the Lord's will? Sure tonight is a heartache. Sure we're all grieving. But I'll tell you this, I'd grieve more if we lost the hospital.

SOUND: *Crowd reaction.*

Do you want to know what kind of medical care the likes of us would get without her? I'll tell you. NOTHING! So, put your rocks down, and go home. We'll never have a better doctor. Don't be making her go away!

SOUND: *Mumbling crowd disperses and exits.*

ZAC. They're going! They're going.

> ELIZABETH *dashes to catch* SEAN.

ELIZABETH. Wait! Wait!

ZAC *exits, as* ELIZABETH *catches up with* SEAN *on the street.*

SEAN. Why, it's the little doctor herself. Sorry about that ruckus.

ELIZABETH. Thank you! Thank you for stopping that mob! You saved the Infirmary.

SEAN. Now don't be letting them scare you away.

ELIZABETH. It takes more than a shovel and a stone to scare a Blackwell!

SEAN (*trying to explain*). They just never saw a lady doctor before.

ELIZABETH (*firm*). They're going to see more of us! More and more. Just like me.

SEAN. Begging your pardon, Dr. Blackwell. Not like you. There's only one like you! (*Tips his cap.*) Evening, Doctor.

SEAN *exits, as* NARRATORS *enter.*

NARRATOR ONE. It wasn't the first time Dr. Blackwell was threatened.

NARRATOR TWO. And it wasn't the last.

ELIZABETH. Because the real sickness is prejudice! And until I conquer that, I can never stop!

ELIZABETH *and* NARRATORS *exit.* ❧

Responding to Cluster Two

What makes a hero?

Thinking Skill ANALYZING

1. **Analyze,** or examine closely, the main characters in this cluster by listing three of their strongest qualities, attitudes, or abilities. Use your analysis to decide which character or person you most admire as a hero.

Name	Qualities, Attitudes, or Abilities
Alice	
Christy's mother	
Christy	
Crazy Horse	
Sir Bors	
Elizabeth Blackwell	

2. In "Tough Alice," the White Queen says, "Laughter in the face of certain death? It is the very definition of the Hero." Do you agree with this definition? Why or why not?

3. Ian Frazier gives many reasons why Crazy Horse is his personal hero. Which reason do you think makes the strongest support for his case?

4. Why do you think Sir Bors spares the life of Sir Priadan in "Sir Bors Fights for a Lady"?

5. Analyze the use of the chorus in "Elizabeth Blackwell: Medical Pioneer." What is the purpose of this group?

Writing Activity: Short and Sweet

Write a short (one- to two-page) action-packed story with a hero. Use some of the qualities, attitudes, or abilities from the analysis chart of question one above. Share your final product with an audience.

A Strong Short Story

- develops at least two characters: a protagonist and an antogonist
- uses dialogue for maximum impact
- contains a conflict
- ends with a resolution of the conflict

CLUSTER THREE

Hero or Not?

Thinking Skill EVALUATING

Hero's Return

KRISTIN HUNTER

I tell you, I was about to explode, I was so excited when I heard my big brother Junior was coming home.

Junior spent eighteen months in the House.[1] He took out a long stretch, cause somebody shot off a gun the day Junior and his corner boys held up the Kravitz's ice-cream store. Nobody got hurt, but Mrs. Kravitz hollered like somebody had killed her. The others got away, and Junior caught the whole blame. It was enough to put him away for a long, long time.

My corner boys were real impressed when I told them. Course they acted like it wasn't nothing, like any one of them could do eighteen months standing on his head. But they were impressed right on, and jealous besides, not having a brother like Junior or anybody else famous in the family.

I remember the headline—"Aging Couple Robbed"—and Junior's picture in the paper. I cut it out and saved it. It's still in my snapshot album that I never did put any other pictures in cause I never got the camera. My brother was big stuff. Front-page stuff. And now he was coming home.

Josh he acted like it weren't nothing. "Eighteen months?" he said. "What's that? I hear you get you own TV in the House, and your own room."

No ghetto kid has his own room, except me after Junior went away. And now he was coming home, and me glad to share it with him again.

"Yeah," says Marquis, "I hear tell they have ice cream every night up there. Double scoops on Sundays. And people come around and give them cigarettes, things like that."

---

1 **House:** slang term for jail

ARRANGEMENT IN GREEN
1993
Allan M. Burch

We only used to get ice cream when we found enough soda bottles to return to the store. And now they got those No Deposit No Return bottles, we don't hardly ever get none unless somebody's Mom gives him a dime. If she does, you got to run all the way home to eat it by yourself, else fight some bigger kids for it. And even if you get past the big guys, there's *your* boys, Josh and Duke and Leroy and Marquis, all wanting to take turns licking off your ice-cream cone.

"Man, I ain't studying no ice cream," said Leroy. He acts like he's the baddest thing on McCarter Street just cause he's thirteen and the rest of us is only twelve. "I could use some cigarettes, though."

This was one time I was with Leroy. I don't think about ice cream much no more cause I don't like to go in Kravitz's store since it happened. I favor my brother in the face,[2] and old Mrs. Kravitz might start yelling her head off again. You can get cigarettes anywhere.

But we don't never have enough money, unless King or one of the other big-time hustlers[3] on the corner gives us some to run an errand. The other hustlers only give us fifty cents, but sometimes King gives a whole dollar. I seen him take a roll of money thick as my fist out of his pocket plenty of times.

We were standing around that July morning, waiting for King to show up, hoping he would give one of us something to do. We all want to be hustlers when we grow up. A hustler is somebody who lives by his wits, you might say, and King was the king of them all.

It was hot enough to boil water on the sidewalk that morning, and my foot was blistered from a hole in my sneaks. I was thinking, Maybe when Junior gets home he'll pull off another job and get me a new pair, when King glides up to the curb in his white air-conditioned Hog.

The Cadillac was about half a block long, and a sharp fox in a blonde wig was sitting beside King. He looked cool as an ice cube in there, his wavy hair shining and diamonds flashing on his hands.

"Hey, you boy. Come here!" He flicked a little button in the Hog, and the window slid down easy as greased silk. Josh and Duke and Leroy and Marquis all hit the sidewalk, but I had a head start in my sneakers, hole and all. I got to the car a full three feet ahead of them.

Then—man!—King shoved the girl out of the car and held open the door for *me*. I hopped in and closed the door, and we eased away from

2 **favor . . . in the face:** look like another person
3 **hustlers:** people who aggressively sell or promote something

the curb. Leroy and Josh and Duke and Marquis were left standin' there with their mouths hangin' open.

"Have a cigarette, kid," King said, and handed me a pack of Marlboros with the top flipped up. But what was inside didn't look like no Marlboros. The paper was pink and it had been rolled by hand.

King handed me the dashboard lighter. I lit up and held the smoke in.

King lit a real Marlboro and leaned back, steering the Hog through tight traffic with one hand. "Kid," he said, "you got to the car first, so you must be the most ambitious one on the corner. You want to get ahead in this world?"

I nodded. I couldn't speak cause the smoke had me all choked up inside.

"Well," King said, "how'd you like to be my right-hand man?"

"Yes!" I cried.

"All you got to do," King said, "is pass this stuff out among the kids." And he pulls a plastic bag out from under the seat. "When they want more, you come back to me. I'll tell you what to charge 'em."

And then King pulled that big old wad out of his pocket and plucked off a crisp new five and handed it to me. My eyes popped. But I didn't lose my cool. Just sat back and inhaled that pink cigarette like a man.

It was making me feel like a man too. Like I could do anything. I put the five in the pocket of my jeans and sucked in the smoke and held it in like I seen Leroy do one time. I felt ten feet tall, higher than high. Way above the funky scuffling people we were cruising by on Madison.

"Man," I said to King, "this is some good stuff."

"Oughta be. It came all the way from Panama," King said. "Listen, kid. The cops don't exactly dig this action, you understand?"

"I'm hip," I said.

"Don't let any of 'em catch you with it. And don't smoke it all yourself, neither."

"Don't worry, King. I'll take care of business," I told him.

"Good," King said and grinned. The wrinkles in his handsome face sank in and made it look like a skull. "You were the one I wanted, kid, you know that? I just didn't know your name."

That made me feel good, but at the same time I got a funny feeling in the stomach. Like when I've had some corn chips and a cherry soda and Mom puts a big platter on the table and I can't eat.

King was waving at people and honking his horn. Everybody stopped what they were doing and waved back. King's the biggest man in town.

Everybody wants to know him. And there *I* was, riding right beside him.

Then we turned sharp into McCarter, and there on the corner was Junior. Thinner than when I saw him last, and with dark smudges under his eyes. But he was *home.*

"I got to get out now, King," I said. "That's my brother over there." Junior looked up and saw me.

"Jody!" he cried and took a step toward me. I had meant to shake hands, the way men do, but instead I flew at him and we hugged right there on the street. My head used to just hit the middle of his chest, but now it touched his chin.

We stepped back, kind of embarrassed, and shook hands like I had meant to do in the first place.

"Boy," he said, "you must've grown a foot. Keep it up, you be tall as me."

And he laughed and rubbed my head. But his eyes were all squinched up like he was trying to keep tears back. I didn't like to see him looking like that, so I started talking fast.

"Did they treat you all right at the House, Junior? I bet you made 'em respect you. I bet they knew you weren't no one to mess with. Didn't they, Junior?"

"I don't want to talk about it," he said. "What were you doing in that car?"

The big Hog with the special-made front license plate, *K I N G,* was still parked at the corner.

"Tell you later," I said, though I was busting to tell him then. "I want to hear how you made out in the slammer."

"Let's get home," he said. But before we could, Duke and Leroy and Josh and Marquis came running up. They surrounded us and pelted Junior with questions.

"Did they give you a TV, man?"

"How was the food? Good?"

"Who'd you meet in there? Any of the big cats?"

"Yeah, I bet you got connections now. I bet you ready for the big time."

Them guys. Sometimes I wish they would leave a guy alone. But they my boys, and they was as excited to see him as I was.

Junior just kept steady walkin', his mouth set in a tight line, saying nothing to the guys until they gave up and fell back. We got to our building. And there over the door was a big cardboard sign Mom had lettered in crayon: WELCOME HOME SON. Just like they do for the heroes that come back from Vietnam.

Junior stood and stared at the sign for a minute. Then he stepped over the kids that are always hanging around out front and yanked the sign down. He ripped it in four pieces and dropped it in the gutter.

"Junior!" I hollered. "What you want to do that for? You'll make Mom feel bad."

"I already made her feel bad," he said. "Come on." He pushed me ahead of him into the hallway.

"You didn't even speak to nobody," I complained. "Josh and Leroy and them, and your old ace Tom Cat, and old Mr. Baltimore. And Mrs. Walters. She was sittin' in the front window like always. You didn't even speak to *her*. They all want to see you, Junior. They been askin' about you while you been away."

"I spoke to *you,* didn't I?" he said. "Which door is it?"

Our building has so many apartments in it I lost count. Still, it was kind of a shock that Junior didn't remember his own apartment door. Made me realize how long he'd been away. And how far, even though you can reach the House by the number 14 bus.

"One more flight up," I told him. When we got there I didn't have to give him any more directions.

Mom was standing in the door with her arms held out in welcome. Junior tried to push past her and get inside, but she had to give him a hug and have her a cry right there. People from the other apartments were watching. I was embarrassed, so I pushed between Mom and Junior and got through the door. That separated them.

Mom stepped back into the apartment. Junior followed her and shut the door real quick behind him. He locked all the locks, the bolt and the chain lock and the police lock that goes right down into the floor. Like he didn't want to ever let anybody in again.

"Lord, child, let me look at you," Mom said when she had dried her eyes on her apron. "Looks like you didn't hardly get enough to eat in that place."

That bothered me some, to tell you the truth. It wasn't at all like what Leroy and them had been saying. But maybe it was just that Junior had lost all his baby fat and was getting lean and hard.

He stood there in the middle of the floor like he hadn't really come to stay and was planning to leave any second. It kept Mom from fussing over him anymore. She started fussing over the stove instead, measuring rice and stirring the chicken and okra. Man! It sure smelled delicious. Suddenly I was real hungry.

"Stewed chicken and okra tonight, honey," she said to Junior. "Your favorite supper. And later I got some people coming in who want to see my son."

"I don't want to see any people," Junior said. "I'm kind of tired. I'm going to take me a little rest."

And without another word he went into our room and shut the door.

"Anything you say, son," Mom said. But he didn't hear her. He had already slammed the bedroom door.

Pretty soon she started crying again. I couldn't stand that, so I took a beer out of the ice box and went to the room and knocked.

"Is that you, Jody?"

"Yes."

"Come in."

"I thought you might like a beer," I said, shutting the door behind me.

"Thanks," he said and took it. He didn't say any more, just lay on his back on his bed, staring at the ceiling. I sat on the edge of my bed and watched him for a while. The room was getting tenser by the minute.

"Planning a job, huh?" I finally said.

"I can't get a job. I've got a record."

"I mean a *big-time* job," I said. "Like you pulled off at Kravitz's, only bigger."

He rolled over and looked at me for the first time. "You think I'm a hero, don't you?" he said. "A big-shot crook. Like in the movies."

"Sure, Junior," I said eagerly. "All the guys do. They expect you to do great things. You got the connections and the smarts now. You must know a lot more than when you went in the House. You was only seventeen then. Now you're a man."

"Yeah, I'm a man," Junior said disgustedly, "and ain't a thing in this town I can do. Nobody's going to hire a jailbird."

"It's all right," I said. "I can take care of us for a while, till you get yourself together."

I pulled out the five and showed it to him.

He was up on his feet, standing over me. "Where'd you get that?"

Something in his manner scared me, but I went on. "King gave it to me. And I'm going to make a lot more. Selling this." I pulled the plastic bag out of my pocket. "It's—"

"I know what it is," Junior said and took off his belt. "Go flush it down the toilet."

"But, Junior—"

He gave me a whack with the back of his hand. It caught me by surprise and sent me sprawling on the floor.

"Flush it, I said. And come right back here when you finished."

I trembled, 'cause I knew what was coming. He had the belt in his hand, folded over double. My face was stinging from the whack, and I was beginning to cry, more from surprise than anything else. But on my way to the bathroom and back I didn't let Mom see me.

Junior was waiting for me when I got back. "So you want to go to jail, huh? All right, I'll show you what jail is like."

He locked the door from the inside and gave me the worst whipping I ever had in my life. The only one, in fact. Pop left home before I was born, and Mom was always too kindhearted to beat us. She had heard me yelling and was at the door, banging on it to be let in. "Junior, what's going on in there? What you doing to my baby?"

"Saving him, that's what," Junior yelled back through the door. "If he ain't already ruint."

He didn't open the door, either. He went right on whipping me. When he was through, he said, "You going to stay away from that slick hustler, huh? You going to stay off that corner and leave those pint-size hoods alone?"

I didn't answer, I was so mad.

"All right. You got a week to think about it." He shut the door behind him and locked me in.

"What you doing to my baby?" Mom cried again.

Junior said, "He wants to go to jail. So let him try it for a few days. Let him live on bread and water and stay in solitary and get knocked around every time he opens his mouth."

Mom let out a wail that sounded like a police siren, but it didn't change Junior's mind. He brought me bread and water for supper and took out the mattresses so he could sleep on them in the front room. *I* would sleep on the springs and get a taste of what a prison bed was like.

He explained it all to me patiently, like he wasn't angry anymore. "The small-time crooks, they get to talk to each other. But the real big-time criminals like you get solitary. And if they *real* bad actors, the guards take the springs out of the cell too. Then they sleep on the floor. I'm your guard. And if you a bad actor, I get to knock you around. Understand?"

But that was all he would say. Once or twice he knocked me around a little, just to show me it wasn't a game. The rest of the time, he didn't say or do nothing. Just brought the bread and water and took me to the bathroom.

I got so lonesome in there I wished he would come in, even to beat me. The old bedsprings stuck me no matter which way I turned, so I lay on the floor, thinking about stewed chicken and okra and having cramps in my belly. All I had to listen to was their arguments.

"You gonna kill him," Mom said.

"No," Junior told her. "He might get killed in jail. That happens to lots of guys. But this way he's gonna live."

"He's only a baby," she wailed.

"He's big enough to get in big trouble. I got home just in time."

The first night wasn't so bad. I expected Mom to come to my rescue any minute. But he wouldn't let her. In the morning I heard her going off to work. They would fire her if she took off two days in a row, so she had to go.

The second and third days, I lay there trying to remember boss things I'd done with the guys, like chasing girls in the park and stealing fruit and sneaking rides on the back of trucks. But pretty soon those things bored me too.

On the fourth day, I got some of my school books down from the closet and began reading. I even got interested in history.

Junior came in while I was lying on my stomach with the book open on the floor in front of me. For a scary moment I thought he was going to take it away. But he just looked at me. And then he smiled.

"Gonna be a big-time criminal like me?"

"No."

"Gonna drop out of school like I did?"

"No." I paused and thought very carefully, then surprised myself by what I said. "I think I might go to that tutoring place at Mom's church and make up math. I think I could pass it this time."

"What I think," Junior said, "is you ready to come out now. I'm gonna parole[4] you. But you got to watch your step, you hear? No associating with known criminals. No messing up. A single slip, and back you go."

Then he fixed me a big breakfast. He explained that since we didn't have a father anymore, he had to be the man of the house. It made him feel good, he said, knowing at least part of what he had to do.

Then he let me go out on the street.

It looked different, like a place I hadn't seen in years and years. With all the slick people and crooks and hustlers, it looked like a place where

---

4 **parole:** conditional release of a prisoner

I didn't want to stay very long.

"Hey, man," Leroy hollered at me, "where you been?"

I was still weak and wobbly in spite of the breakfast. But I felt stronger and older than Leroy and the others. I knew things they still had to learn. One thing I knew was if I ever made it off that corner, I would have to make it alone.

"I been," I said, "in jail."

Then I left them and went on my way, knowing where I was going and walking like a man. ∾

A Couple of Really Neat Guys

DAVE BARRY

If you were to ask me how I came to be running after litterbugs in downtown Miami while wearing bright-red women's tights, I would have to say that the turning point was a visit to my optometrist.[1]

My optometrist is named Dr. Jeffrey Jeruss, and although he looks like a normal human being, only slightly larger, it turns out that when it comes to littering he is—and I mean this as a compliment—insane. So am I. I HATE littering. I hate it when you go to a park or the beach and the day is suddenly destroyed by the arrival of: The Picnic People from Hell. You know these people. They have a large nuclear-powered radio and enough food to supply several Canadian provinces, and they immediately transform themselves into a high-output litter machine, cranking out potato-chip bags and beer cans and sandwich wrappers and chicken bones and dirty diapers weighing more than the infant that generated them.

And when it's time to leave, these people simply . . . leave. They pick nothing up. They just WALK AWAY from what looks like the scene of a tragic dumpster explosion. And on the way home flick their cigarette butts out of the car window. Of course! You wouldn't want to mess up a sharp-looking ashtray interior, not when the entire planet is available! Ha ha! Good thinking, you SLIME-EXCRETING MORONS. WHY DON'T YOU TAKE YOUR CIGARETTE BUTTS AND—

Forgive me. I get carried away. But I never did anything about it except mutter and seethe until my fateful visit to Dr. Jeruss for an eye exam. He was shining his little light into my eyeballs and making that "hmmmmm"

---

1 **optometrist:** a trained specialist who corrects vision problems

noise that doctors are trained to make, when I happened to mention littering. Suddenly Jeffrey started stomping around the examination room, neck muscles bulging, denouncing the beer-can tossers of the world and waving his eyeball light around like the Hammer of Thor.[2] Watching him, I realized that I had finally found the perfect sidekick for: Captain Tidy.

Captain Tidy is a concept I have fantasized about for many years. He is a masked avenger for the forces of neatness. When a person litters, Captain Tidy comes swooping out of nowhere and explains to the litterer, in polite terms, that he or she is being a jerk. What kept me from acting out this fantasy was the fear of being embarrassed, by which I mean having my nose punched into my brain. But I knew that if Captain Tidy had a SIDEKICK, a LARGE sidekick, a large, TRAINED OPTOMETRIST sidekick, that would be a whole different story.

And thus Jeff and I became: Captain Tidy and Neatness Man. We assembled costumes consisting of the aforementioned red tights (size triple-extra large), plus red Superman-style boots, plus blue shorts and shirts with our superhero names professionally lettered on them, plus white gloves, plus capes made from garbage bags, plus utility belts from which were suspended feather dusters, dustpans and rubber gloves.

Also, of course, we wore hoods and masks to preserve our Secret Identities. If you had seen us wearing our outfits and standing in our official superhero stance—hands on hips, chest thrust out, garbage bags blowing out dramatically behind—your only possible reaction would have

2 **Hammer of Thor:** The ancient Norse god, Thor, used a hammer as a tool to create lightning and as a weapon to throw at his enemies.

been to say, with genuine emotion in your voice, "What a pair of dorks."

But we didn't care. We were on a mission. We rented a black Tidymobile with very dark windows, and we spent a day cruising the streets. When we saw people litter, we'd leap out, rush up to the perpetrators, pick up their litter, hand it back to them and say, with deep but polite superhero voices, "Sir, you don't want to litter, DO YOU?" Inevitably, they'd look ashamed, take their litter back and dispose of it properly. One possible explanation for this, of course, is that they thought we were dangerous escaped perverted tights-wearing lunatics. But I like to think that they were genuinely impressed with our message. At one point, a tough-looking street crowd actually APPLAUDED us for making a man pick up his cigarette butt. And remember, this was in MIAMI, a city where armed robbery is only a misdemeanor.[3]

By the end of the day, thanks to our efforts, Miami had been transformed from a city with crud all over the streets into a city with crud all over the streets. But at least SOME litterers had been chastised, and Jeff and I felt a LOT better. I strongly recommend that you consider becoming a litter avenger in your particular city or town or random suburban area. What's the worst that could happen to you? OK, death. But probably you'd do fine. Just remember to be polite. "Speak softly and carry a large sidekick"—that's Rule Two of the Captain Tidy Code. Rule One, of course, is: "Always visit the bathroom BEFORE you put on your tights." ∾

---

3 **misdemeanor:** minor crime

Time for a Hero

BRIAN M. THOMSEN

The man on the table began to stir.

Good. He's coming around. He's our only hope!

The two doctors in attendance immediately positioned themselves on each side of him, as he blinked his eyes, and began to regain consciousness.

"Thank God you're alright," offered the older doctor. "We didn't know what to do. Why, if you hadn't come around, we would have had to . . . "

"Of course he came around," the younger doctor interrupted. "He's never failed us before."

"Where am I?" said the patient, trying to shake off the last strains of grogginess. "What happened?"

"You're in a special mobile military hospital. I'm Doctor Kirschenbaum," said the older doctor. "The marines brought you here right after you passed out. I've been watching you for the past two hours hoping you'd come around. It's not as if we could treat you or anything, given your advanced physiology[1] and all."

" . . . But we knew you'd come around," continued the other. "I'm Dr. Parker, and we knew that it would take more than a direct hit on the forehead from a bazooka shell to stop you."

"Huh?" said the patient, not quite sure if he was really coming around or just trapped in some bizarre waking dream.

"The bazooka shell," repeated Parker. "Don't you remember?"

"No. I don't remember anything. This all must be some dream. Getting hit in the head would kill an ordinary man . . . probably blow him to bits. No,

---

1 **physiology:** a body's characteristics

I'm just not awake yet. This is all just a dream," he added, the pounding in his head becoming more and more noticeable. "I'm going to just close my eyes, go back to sleep, and wake up later when I'm not so delirious."

"You can't do that," insisted Dr. Kirschenbaum. "We need you. Surely you must remember the crisis . . . your mission . . . what you have to do . . ."

"What do I have to do?" he asked, hoping that this dream would soon be over.

"Save the world, of course," answered Parker.

"Save the world?" he repeated.

"Of course," Kirschenbaum insisted. "You must remember. So many lives are at stake."

"I don't even remember my name," the patient realized, now painfully awake and aware of his own befuddlement.

The two doctors were shocked.

"He doesn't remember his name," Parker said to Kirschenbaum.

"He doesn't remember his mission," Kirschenbaum said to Parker; then, after a brief inspiration added, "You don't suppose he has amnesia,[2] do you?"

"It could be," Parker said. "A hard blow to the head of a normal man could lead to amnesia. A blow such as one from a bazooka shell to a head such as his . . . who could tell?"

"Wait a second," the patient insisted, interrupting their consultation. "Why do you say 'a normal man'?"

"I'm sorry," apologized Parker. "Maybe I should have said a mortal man, or an Earthman, or . . ."

"Well, what am I then?" the patient insisted, anger replacing his confusion.

"He really doesn't know who he is," Kirschenbaum said to no one in particular, perhaps to himself, perhaps to his patient.

"Who am I?" he demanded, the threat of violence barely masked in his voice.

"Why, you're Meteor Man," Kirschenbaum answered, "and time is running out, and you have to save the world."

▲ ▲ ▲

For the next few minutes, Doctors Parker and Kirschenbaum carefully reassured the patient known as Meteor Man of his real identity.

2 **amnesia:** loss of memory

They told him the now-famous origin story that had been immortalized in comic books, cartoons, and Sunday features, of how a meteor fell from the sky, and after seven days of cooling cracked open, giving birth to a super-infant, hatched like a chick from an egg. Raised in secret by a retired five-star general and his wife, the super-infant matured and eventually became Meteor Man, strength of a thousand, indestructible, and savior of the planet.

"Surely you must remember the time you averted disaster by extending the course of the Missouri River to put out the raging fires in southern Oregon?" insisted Dr. Parker.

"Or the time you outwitted the deadly brain-stealing ETs from Alpha Centauri?" added Kirschenbaum.

"Or when you single-handedly shielded all of Las Vegas from an atomic bomb blast when you smothered the explosion with your own body," continued Parker, adding, "and lived."

"And lived?" repeated the patient known as Meteor Man, in disbelief.

"Of course," added Dr. Kirschenbaum; then, chuckling, he said, "And who'd have thought a little thing like a bazooka shell would cause amnesia?"

"I don't believe any of this!" said the patient.

"But you have to," said Kirschenbaum calmly. "You've never failed us before, and you are our only hope."

A strange sense of well-being seemed to wash over the confused patient. *Our only hope.* It sounded so familiar . . . but who could believe these fantastic tales of his exploits? And no one in the real world would ever be called Meteor Man. Either he was now in the hands of delusionary[3] madmen, the victim of some bizarre practical joke, or he himself had gone crazy . . . or, there was one other alternative, most bizarre of all—maybe they were right. He was *their only hope.* The whole phrase felt right . . . but it couldn't be.

Trying to maintain a certain nonthreatening calm, the patient responded to his doctors.

"Look," he offered, "I'd like to help, and I'd do anything I could to save the world, but I'm just one man."

"More than a man," interrupted Parker.

"Whatever," he responded, quickly tiring of the annoying little doctor's interruptions, and clarifications. "But what is the crisis, and what can I do about it?"

"We've just received an update from our men on the front," answered

---

3 **delusionary:** holding false beliefs

Kirschenbaum, now all businesslike and efficient. "The terrorist forces guarding the plant have been subdued by a black-beret insurgency team,[4] casualties listed at seventy-five percent."

"An acceptable number, given the situation," said the annoying Dr. Parker, adding, "so you have nothing to worry about from those migraine-inducing bazookas for the time being."

"We've since discovered that they've planted an Alunarium bomb, which when detonated will create an implosion[5] that will generate a black hole instigating China Syndrome[6] at an almost instantaneous rate which will tear the Earth asunder from core to crust."

"And what can I do about it?" asked the patient known as Meteor Man.

"It's really quite simple," replied Kirschenbaum, producing a mechanical box not unlike an old-fashioned Geiger counter. "All you have to do is carry this magnetic wave transmitter into the plant. The waves will erase the programming of the Alunarium bomb, making detonation impossible."

"What's the catch?" asked Meteor Man, knowing that one had to exist.

"There isn't any catch, at least not for you," answered Parker.

Kirschenbaum explained, "The terrorists flooded the plant area with the coolant from the atomic core. The intense levels of radioactivity would kill any of us, but you're immune."

Parker added, "I remember your comment to the press when you smothered the atomic bomb. You said, 'I feel like I've been out in the sun a bit too long.' Isn't that a scream! A lethal dose of radiation to us gives you a mild case of sunstroke. Walking into the contaminated plant should be a piece of cake."

"You expect me to believe I'm impervious[7] to radiation," said the patient.

"Of course," said the annoying Parker. "You're Meteor Man."

Parker gestured towards the patient's chest.

The patient looked down, and for the first time noticed the large M insignia that covered most of his chest. He seemed to be wearing some sort of garish costume made out of a spandex-like material that hugged the contours of his muscularly masculine physique with a sheen of gold and silver.

His first thought was that he looked like something out of a comic

---

4 **black-beret insurgency team:** group trained to deal with those who might revolt against authority; this group characterized by wearing black, flat caps

5 **implosion:** a violent, inward collapse

6 **China Syndrome:** the theory that a nuclear meltdown could sink through the earth to reach China

7 **impervious:** untouchable; immune

book, but then he caught himself before he said anything, realizing that this would have been just the sort of reaction Parker and Kirschenbaum would have wanted.

"I suppose this is my costume?" he commented.

"Known by one and all," replied Parker. "The savior of mankind, and our only hope in our darkest and direst times of need."

"But dressing in a costume," he added, "doesn't necessarily mean I am some sort of superhero who can fly through the air, leap tall bridges, see through walls . . ."

"You can't do any of those things," Kirschenbaum interrupted. "Your body is impervious to damage from bullets, radiation waves, laser beams . . ."

"But not direct hits on the forehead by bazooka shells," he added.

"Apparently," Kirschenbaum conceded, "your recuperative stamina[8] is one hundred times that of a mortal man. Your strength is that of a thousand, your intellect is off the IQ chart . . ."

"I don't feel like a genius."

"It's probably a by-product of the amnesia," offered the annoying Parker. "I wouldn't worry about that."

"I somehow figured you wouldn't," he replied curtly.

Kirschenbaum looked at his watch and became more concerned.

"Meteor Man," he said gravely, "we are running out of time. I know you are confused, and it all sounds far-fetched, but you are our only hope, and time is running out. What do I have to do to convince you that you are who we say you are?"

Meteor Man was touched by his earnestness and concern. If time was running out, and he was their only hope, then he would have to do something . . . but what if they were wrong? He didn't feel like some sort of meteor-spawn from outer space.

"Dr. Kirschenbaum," he offered, "I really would like to help you, but it all sounds so bizarre. No sane person would believe that he was some sort of superhero."

"Of course not," interrupted the annoying Dr. Parker. "You're one of a kind. That is why you are our only hope."

Both the patient and Kirschenbaum ignored Parker's latest cliché[9] outburst.

Kirschenbaum considered the situation for a moment, and proposed

8 **recuperative stamina:** ability to recover
9 **cliché:** an overused expression

a solution, saying, "If I can prove to you that you are indeed Meteor Man, our invincible hero, then would you save the day?"

"Sure," said the patient, really wanting to help, and also to regain his identity.

Kirschenbaum raised his hand to his face and lightly brushed his moustache, seeming to be in some sort of intense thought. The glow of inspiration illuminated his face, as if he had just arrived at a solution. Dropping his hand from his face to his chest, he reached into his lab coat, pulled out a .44 Magnum, and quickly fired off five shots point-blank into the chest of the patient he called Meteor Man.

Meteor Man had almost no time to react, taking a quick deep breath as he felt the dull impact of the shells against his chest, not even noticing that instinctively his hand had tried to move to block the bullets' impact.

He felt no pain, no harm.

He was speechless. The bullets had impacted, but had not penetrated.

Looking down at his hand, he felt a peculiar sensation of warmth.

There in the palm of his hand were the five shells, tips slightly flattened and worse for wear from their impact with his chest.

"You see?" said Kirschenbaum. "Bullets bounce off you, and though you don't consciously remember how to use your powers, your body and your subconscious do, as evidenced by your catching the shells at super-speed."

Meteor Man just stared at the still-warm shells in his hand.

"Come here," said Kirschenbaum, continuing his quest to prove to his patient that he was indeed invulnerable. "Please put your hand down here on the table."

Meteor Man dully complied.

Dr. Kirschenbaum then took out a surgical saw, turned it on, and proceeded to file down the high-speed blade on each of the fingers of the patient's right hand. In no time at all, the steel blade was reduced to a pile of metal shavings, while Meteor Man's fingers and skin remained unharmed.

Meteor Man's eyes moved back and forth from his unscathed right hand to the shell-laden palm of his left hand.

Dr. Kirschenbaum guided him over to a telemonitor[10] and said, "Observe." The monitor clicked on.

The Update News Channel was tuned in. A stern-faced anchorman was in the middle of a story:

10 **telemonitor:** display screen for televised or computerized photos and information

". . . there is still no word on the condition of Meteor Man, who was apparently dazed when he was hit in the head by a bazooka shell. The thought-to-be invulnerable hero has faced many greater adversaries before (*visual montage*[11] *of stock news footage of his earlier exploits*), including the now-famous stifling of an atomic bomb that threatened to level Las Vegas. America wishes Meteor Man a speedy recovery . . ."

▲ ▲ ▲

Kirschenbaum hit the control and froze the screen on a head shot of Meteor Man accepting the Medal of Freedom from President Levin.

Meteor Man looked from the monitor's image to the mirror across the room.

The face was the same.

He was Meteor Man.

It was the only possible answer . . . and he was their only possible hope.

He slowly turned back to Dr. Kirschenbaum and said softly, "What do I have to do?"

Kirschenbaum put his arm around the costumed hero's shoulder and said, "Your memory should return in a short time. We can go over video-tapes of your past exploits later to try to jog it back into place. For now, we must avert our immediate crisis."

"The bomb in the plant," he stated.

"Yes. All you have to do is bring this transmitter into the plant itself. That's all. A helicopter is waiting to escort you to the plant. You will be lowered down to the ground by a towline so as not to risk damaging the transmitter. All you have to do is disengage yourself from the line, walk into the plant, through the contaminated puddles, and set it down here." Kirschenbaum pointed to a room on a blueprint that had conveniently appeared on the teleprompter.

"You see," he added, "it's no more than a hundred paces from your drop-off point."

"And that's it?" asked Meteor Man.

"That's it," said Dr. Kirschenbaum. "Then all you have to do is walk on out, come back here, and we can work on filling in the gaps in your memory."

"Once again, the Earth will be saved, by mankind's only hope," said the annoying Parker.

"Right," said the tolerant Meteor Man.

---

11 **montage:** a rapid succession of images

"This is the transmitter. It is always on, so you don't have to do anything to it," instructed Kirschenbaum putting the device into his patient's hands and escorting him to the door, saying, "Your helicopter awaits."

As they were leaving the room, Meteor Man noticed a black beret on a chair by the door. He paused for a moment, picked it up, and was about to put it on and see how it looked in the mirror, when Kirschenbaum gently snatched it out of his hands.

"I don't think that would be a good idea. Some of the members of the team that subdued the terrorists may be around, and they might consider it a bit callous considering their lost buddies, who were not, how shall we say, invulnerable."

"I understand," said Meteor Man, who left the room and continued down the corridor to the awaiting helicopter.

▲   ▲   ▲

Kirschenbaum looked at the beret in his hand.

"That was a close call," said the psychopharmacologist[12] Parker. "Seeing himself in the beret might have brought back a few too many conflicting memories. After all, no matter how many doses of pharmacologicals[13] we inject, it's still impossible to effect a complete past erasure, and restructuring."

"Yes," said psychologist Kirschenbaum.

"At least his task is simple enough. He probably won't even notice any adverse effects until he makes it back here. By then the crisis will have been averted, and he'll be in isolation."

"Where we will let him die in peace," muttered Kirschenbaum.

"Yes, far from the questioning eyes of John Q. Public,"[14] continued Parker. "I really have to hand it to you setting up this program. If anyone had told me that we would be able to make your average, everyday soldier believe he was invulnerable, I would never have believed it. The faked computer-enhanced newscast, the Kevlar body suit, breakaway saw blade. One question: how did he manage to catch the bullets?"

"The bullets were electronically programmed to stop on impact, and activate a miniaturized electromagnet that was tuned to the frequency of a metallic salve that I had coated his left palm with."

---

12   **psychopharmacologist:** doctor who studies the effects of drugs on the mind and behavior

13   **pharmacologicals:** drugs

14   **John Q. Public:** the common man

"Ingenious," exclaimed Parker. "Where did you ever get your idea for PROJECT SUPERHERO?"

"Where else?" said Kirschenbaum. "The comic books."

"Well, it certainly works," said Parker, patting the older doctor on the back. "In less than two hours we can turn an ordinary soldier with human flaws and instincts for self-preservation into a confident and care-free hero with no other concerns except the completion of his mission. One man dies so that many can be saved. No matter how you look at it, that's a more than acceptable casualty rate. Lt. O'Connor, aka[15] Meteor Man I, will get a hero's funeral, and the day will be saved."

"A hero's funeral," mused the increasingly more depressed Dr. Kirschenbaum. "I remember reading about the Soviet firemen who rushed into Chernobyl to contain the fire to keep the plant from explod-ing, knowing that in doing so they were signing their own death warrants. I also remember stories of soldiers earning medals that were awarded posthumously[16] by jumping on top of hand grenades . . ."

"That's where you got your idea for Meteor Man smothering the atomic bomb that would have leveled Las Vegas," Parker added gleefully.

"I guess," responded Kirschenbaum, "but you've missed the point. In the past there was a time for heroes, when extraordinary men responded to extraordinary circumstances. No one could predict it, yet somehow, because of the appearance of a few good men, we always managed to survive. It was a time of heroes, and one always showed up on time."

"Now all we have to do is invent our own," added Parker, "and we never have to worry about one showing up too late. We turned Lt. O'Connor into Meteor Man in under two hours, and averted the crisis with three hours to spare. What more could we want?"

"What more could Lt. O'Connor want?" Kirschenbaum responded sar-donically. "Maybe just a real chance to be a hero, no deceptions, no false bravado. Maybe all he wanted was the chance to give up his life for the common good. Maybe it was his time to be a hero."

"I'd rather not take that risk," said Parker.

"I suppose you wouldn't," replied Kirschenbaum, turning off the mon-itor till the next crisis, until the time arrived when Meteor Man II would make his entrance. ❧

---

15 **aka:** also known as

16 **posthumously:** after death

The Unknown Hero

REBECCA CHRISTIAN

*"Why are you here? You have done nothing but create misery.
My city is in chaos because of you."*

No one knows who he was nor what has become of him. Yet through the power of a single stark photograph, the young Chinese man who spoke these words of passionate outrage on June 5, 1989, has become a symbol around the world.

Slight, ordinary-appearing, simply dressed in black slacks and a thin white shirt, the young man seemed an unlikely hero. He defied his country's army because, in the early morning hours of the previous day, soldiers in the Chinese military had massacred hundreds of people: students, workers, professionals, and even some children. These people were either innocent bystanders or peaceful demonstrators in Beijing's historic Tienanmen Square, significant because it was the scene of the first modern Chinese student protest in 1919. Some of those slaughtered were crushed by tanks; others were shot in the back.

The upheaval had begun several weeks before when a group of college students used the funeral of a government leader as an occasion to demonstrate their anger over slow political reform and government corruption. They also expressed their demands for better jobs, housing, and education along with their hunger for freedom of expression. Several weeks of protests and unrest resulted in the declaration of martial law on May 20th. It culminated in the violence that erupted June 4th, shocking the world and largely silencing the students.

The day after the Tienanmen Square massacre, a column of 18 tanks rumbled down a nearby thoroughfare called the Avenue of Eternal Peace. A treacherous dance began when the young man stepped in front of them. When the lead tank swerved to avoid hitting him, the man blocked it again. The tank turned the opposite direction; so did the man. Then he climbed on the vehicle and spoke the simple but stirring words that assured his place in history.

After he climbed down, others at the scene who were sympathetic surrounded the young rebel and whisked him away. Some think he went into hiding; others insist he was killed. Whatever his fate, the photograph lives on as a potent symbol of one man's courage against oppression. ✑

Responding to Cluster Three

Hero or Not?

Thinking Skill EVALUATING

1. Using a chart such as the one below, list heroic and non-heroic actions of the selections' characters. What makes this person a hero? What might make this person *not* a hero?

Reasons why a hero	Character	Reasons why not a hero
	Junior	
	Litter Heroes	
	Lt. O'Connor ("Meteor Man")	
	Chinese man	

2. In "Hero's Return," **evaluate,** or judge, Junior's treatment of his little brother, Jody. Do you agree with Junior's actions? Why or why not?

3. **Foreshadowing** is a technique authors use to hint at future developments in a story. Look for such hints in "Time for a Hero." Point out at least one place you see foreshadowing.

4. Do you believe that the "unknown hero" was a naive risk-taker or a patriotic hero? Explain your choice.

Writing Activity: Choose a Star

If you were going to make a movie on the topic of heroism, which character from this book would you choose? Explain your choice by evaluating the strengths, weaknesses, and overall heroic qualities of this character.

A Strong Evaluation

• identifies characteristics and criteria

• assesses strong and weak points

• determines value

CLUSTER FOUR

THINKING ON YOUR OWN

Thinking Skill   SYNTHESIZING

Hamish Mactavish Is Eating a Bus

GORDON KORMAN

It was over the Sunday paper that I first learned that a forty-one-year-old man named Hamish Mactavish of Inverness, Scotland, was eating a bus.

The Sunday paper was a family thing at the Donaldson house. Mom and Dad dreamed it up as a weekly ceasefire in the war between me and my worst enemy on earth, that waste of bathroom tissue, my brother, Chase the Disgrace.

Chase and I are twins—not identical, that's for sure. I can't believe we once shared the same womb together. It's all I can bear to be in the same town as the guy, let alone the same house, and three of the same classes. Mom said she experienced a lot of kicking during pregnancy. My theory is that all that action was me trying to strangle Chase with the umbilical cord. I've always been blessed with a good dose of common sense, although I'm not very smart in a school-ish way. Chase got all the academic ability—not to mention the athletic talent, good looks, popularity, and the bigger room, with a view of the mountains, not the garage.

Neither of us could have eaten a bus. That might be the only area Chase didn't have it over me.

"I don't understand why you two can't make a better effort to get along," our mother was always complaining.

Of course *she* didn't understand. She was lucky enough to have been born an only child. She would never accept that we were natural enemies: Lion and antelope; Macintosh and IBM; matter and antimatter; Warren and Chase.

So naturally Chase jumped all over me when I found that tiny little story squeezed between brassiere ads in the wilds of page G27.

"Get out of here!" Chase scoffed. "It's impossible to eat a bus!"

"It's not impossible for Hamish Mactavish," I told him. "He's already half-done with the front fender. So there, pinhead."

"Doofus," Chase countered.

"Idiot."

"Look who's talking—"

"*I'd* like to know how he's doing it," my mother said quickly. "Surely the man can't chew metal and glass."

"I bet he's just eating the body," my father put in. "I mean, nobody could eat a differential."[1]

I held up the short article. "It says here that he cuts the chassis[2] into bite-sized pieces with a hacksaw and swallows them whole. Then the natural acids of his stomach break them down." I turned to Mom. "Can that happen?"

"Over time, I suppose so," she replied dubiously. "This Mactavish fellow certainly must have a strong stomach."

"Strong? He's amazing!" I exclaimed. "I can't believe this didn't make the front page, with a big picture of Hamish Mactavish with what's left of the bus. This guy should be famous!"

"Star of the insane asylum," put in Chase.

I couldn't wait for the six o'clock news. I was positive Hamish Mactavish was going to be the top story. Instead it was something boring about the president. The *president*! I mean, what had he ever eaten? Not so much as a rearview mirror!

Hamish Mactavish wasn't the second story either. Or the third. In fact, he didn't make the news at all. I figured they were waiting for the late-breaking developments to come in over the wire from Scotland. I switched over to CNN, and watched the entire broadcast.

I could hear Chase in the next room laughing at me over the phone on his nightly calls to eighty-five of his nearest and dearest friends. "Yeah, he's been glued to the tube for three and a half hours! Man, talk about stupid. . . ."

And when I went to bed that night, bug-eyed from staring at the TV, I still hadn't heard a single solitary word about Hamish Mactavish.

▲　▲　▲

Kevin Connolly and Amanda Pace were talking about last night's Bulls game when I slipped into my seat next to them in social studies class.

---

1 **differential:** on a vehicle, a set of gears housed in a heavy metal case that transfers power to the wheels

2 **chassis:** the supporting frame of a vehicle

"Michael Jordan was unbelievable!" Amanda raved. "He scored forty and still had enough rebounds and assists for a triple double."

"Yeah," I agreed. "That guy's the Hamish Mactavish of basketball."

"The *who* of basketball?" Kevin asked.

"Don't tell me you've never heard of Hamish Mactavish!" I exclaimed in disbelief. "He's *only* the top-ranked bus eater in the world today!"

"Bus eater?" echoed Amanda.

"He eats buses," I explained. "At least, he's eating one now."

"How much money does he get?" inquired Kevin.

I stared at him. "How should I know?"

"It's important," argued Kevin, who wouldn't even bother to breathe unless he was getting paid for it. "If I was going to eat a bus, I'd expect my agent to cut a monster deal, with a big signing bonus, and a six-figure payoff when I was done."

"He's not doing it for the money—" I began.

But how did I know that Hamish Mactavish wasn't getting paid for his amazing feat? After all, a bus wasn't an extra slice of pizza that you ate because you were too lazy to wrap it up and put it in the refrigerator. It wasn't even like the time Chase swallowed a caterpillar to impress Leticia Hargrove so she'd like him and hate me. This was *huge*!

"Maybe some rich guy is offering a million dollars to anyone who can eat a bus," Kevin speculated. "Or maybe the Scottish government is running out of dump space. They'd pay big bucks to get rid of out-of-use vehicles."

"I think it's more like the Olympics," I told him. "You don't get paid for the actual thing, but afterwards you clean up on endorsements."

"What kind of endorsements?" Amanda asked dubiously.

"Stomach medicines," I suggested. "Can't you picture the TV commercial? 'Hi, I'm Hamish Mactavish. If you think *you* get heartburn, you should see how much eating a bus can upset your stomach. So when a windshield wiper is giving me nausea, I reach for the instant relief of Gas-Away. . . .' "

Kevin looked thoughtful. "I wonder what kind of contract he'd get for that."

"Not as good as Michael Jordan," mused Amanda.

"Don't be so sure," I put in. "I mean, there are hundreds of basketball players. But if you want a guy who can eat a bus, it's Hamish Mactavish or nobody."

I could tell this made a big impression on Kevin. "What a great negotiating position!" he remarked. "Does this Hamish guy need a manager?"

Amanda looked at me with a new respect. "You know, Warren, I never thought of it that way—" Suddenly she tuned me out.

I craned my neck to see what had captured her attention. She was looking at Chase the Disgrace. Chase never just walked into a room; he *made an entrance,* usually surrounded by a couple of his caveman buddies from the football team.

"Hey, Chase."

"What's going on, Chase?"

"What's happening, man?"

My brother slapped his way through the forest of high-fives until he was standing over me. "Are you still babbling about that bus-eating geek?"

The whole class burst out laughing. Not that his comment was so brilliant, or even hilarious. Most of the kids had never even heard of Hamish Mactavish and what he had set out to do. That's just how it was with Chase. He was the big shot, the cool guy, the sports hero, Mr. Popularity. Everything that came out of his mouth was an automatic gem. The football jerks were practically in hysterics. They had to pound each other on the back just to keep from choking.

Most painful of all, Amanda was laughing too, and gazing worshipfully up at my brother's slick grin.

I could feel the crimson bubbling up from my collar until it had taken total possession of my face. "He's not a geek," I muttered tight-lipped.

"Hi, Amanda." The Disgrace shifted his attention to the desk next to mine. "We're going to hit the mall after school. Feel like meeting us?"

If I was Hamish Mactavish's son, maybe people in our school wouldn't be so impressed by a big phony like Chase. I mean, Amanda practically bit off her tongue promising that right after school she'd run home and get her bike. But, then again, if I was a Mactavish kid, Chase would be, too. And he'd *still* be better than me at absolutely everything.

That really burned me up. Even in my own fantasy, I couldn't get the best of Chase. In a rage, I stood up and threw my pen at him as he high-fived the rest of the way to his desk. The ballpoint whizzed past his shoulder and landed in the fish tank. Chase wheeled and bounced a pencil sharpener with deadly accuracy off my nose. Chase was also a star pitcher during baseball season.

"Let's take it easy on the brotherly love today," suggested Mr. Chin, as he set his briefcase on the desk. "Now, this morning I promised we'd talk about the oral presentations. This semester the subject will be your hero, or the person you admire most. It can be someone you know, or even a figure from history. Warren Donaldson—" suddenly, the teacher's sharp eyes were on me. "This will be fifty percent of your grade. I think you'd bother to take a few notes."

Scattered snickers buzzed through the room. I snuck a look over at the bottom of the fish tank, where the algae eater was nuzzling my pen.

"That's okay, Mr. Chin," I announced. "I already know who my subject is going to be."

▲   ▲   ▲

It wasn't easy doing research on Hamish Mactavish. There must have been some kind of media blackout over in Scotland. There was nothing about him in any of the papers, and the radio and TV news programs were all about senators, and murderers, and embezzlers, and people who got killed in sewer pipe explosions.

"When are you going to face facts?" Chase taunted me. "Nobody cares about Hamish What's-his-face except you!" The doorbell rang. "Oh, that must be Amanda. We're going to the mall."

"The guys who *built* the mall didn't spend as much time there as you two," I snapped at him.

Amanda poked her head around the corner and waved. "Hi, Warren."

I buried my face in my Hamish Mactavish scrapbook and pretended to be too busy to reply. In reality, I still had only the one tiny article from between the brassiere ads—with fifty percent of my social studies grade hanging in the balance.

Did I give up? Would Hamish Mactavish have given up? Never!

The computer database in our school library found another piece on Hamish Mactavish. Okay, it was from fourteen years ago, and I had to go to the public library to get it—not the branch library near where we lived, but the main building downtown. But I was psyched. Even the forty-five-minute train ride couldn't dampen my enthusiasm. I had unearthed another piece of the puzzle that was Hamish Mactavish.

It took all four research librarians, including the chief, who was about ninety, to find what I was looking for. My hands were shaking as I opened the June 1983 issue of *U.K. Adventurer* magazine. It turned out that my Hamish Mactavish, then twenty-seven, became the toast[3] of the British Isles when he ate a grand piano, bench and all. It was an awesome achievement, but, I now knew, just a training mission for bigger and better things to come.

I squinted at the small picture of Mr. Mactavish, who was posed with

---

3 **toast:** an honored or highly admired person

a napkin around his neck, and the final piano key in his mouth. He was a pretty weird-looking guy, with wild, almost bulging eyes, and a dazed expression. He was mostly bald, but several long strands of jet black hair hung down his forehead like jungle vines. He also seemed a little on the fat side, with rosy apple cheeks. I guess pianos are pretty high in calories.

Just looking at him, it came to me in a moment of perfect clarity: A guy like that would *have* to eat a bus if he expected to get any attention in this world! Especially if he had to compete with people like Chase.

The chief librarian gawked over my shoulder. "Good Lord, what kind of creature is that?"

"A role model," I answered without hesitation.

▲ ▲ ▲

"I don't understand why you didn't go to the mall with Chase and Amanda," my mother nagged me.

I was absorbed in pasting the second article in my Hamish Mactavish scrapbook. "They didn't want me," I said without looking up.

She stared at me. "Yes, they did. They *asked* you to go!"

"They were lying."

Mom shook her head. "What is the problem between you two?"

"We have irreconcilable differences," I said stubbornly.

She folded her arms in front of her. "What irreconcilable differences?"

"We hate each other," I told her. "You can't get more irreconcilable than that."

"Open your eyes, Warren," she insisted. "Who put Vicks VapoRub in Chase's toothpaste? Who poured ketchup on the cat the day Chase was try-ing out his new BB gun? Who called the police and reported the car stolen the day of the big tennis championship so we all got arrested, and Chase missed his match? Poor Chase doesn't hate anybody! It's you who have declared all-out war on your brother, who has never done anything to you!"

"He's done something to me," I shot right back. "He's done a lot of somethings to me. Every time Chase draws a breath it just points out how much more brains, talent, good looks, and athletic ability he has than I do. Compared to all that, I'd say I'm pretty innocent!"

At that moment, the side door flew open, and Chase bounded into the kitchen—*in his underwear!* "I'll kill him!" he seethed.

Mom's eyes bulged. "Where are your pants?"

I looked casually out the kitchen window. Chase's bike leaned against the garage, with his jeans still attached to the seat. I struggled to contain the smile that was crystalizing inside of me. I had applied just the right amount of Krazy Glue.

Best of all, Amanda was nowhere to be seen.

▲ ▲ ▲

"Good thing he took off his pants instead of ripping them," Kevin said at school the next day. "Otherwise your parents would probably make you pay for a new pair."

"It still would have been worth it," I assured him. "You should've seen the look on his face. It was like the day he threw that big interception with three seconds to play."

Loyal brother that I am, I've never missed one of Chase's football games. Of course, I always sit in the Visitors bleachers and root for the other team. I can usually work the opposing fans into a pretty good chorus of:

Chase! Chase!
He's a disgrace!
Knock that ugly face
Into outer space!

My family spent a lot of time trying to figure out how all the other teams seemed to develop the same chant.

"Hi, Kevin." Amanda slipped into her seat. She gave me a dirty look.

I know I should have been upset. But I just couldn't shake the image of Chase riding up to the mall beside Amanda, and then trying to get off his bike. He had probably struggled a little—imperceptibly at first, then with increasing effort until his front tire was bouncing up and down on the pavement.

AMANDA: *What's wrong, Chase?*

CHASE: *Uh . . . just checking the air in my tires . . . (more bouncing, becoming violent)*

Kevin sensed the tension and decided to change the subject. "I've been thinking of some marketing angles for Hamish Mactavish. How about this: A coast-to-coast bus trip where he actually eats the bus in different cities as he goes along. He could roll into the L.A. Colliseum on just the motor and four wheels, and scarf down the chassis in front of fifty thousand screaming fans. I call it 'The Hamish Mactavish Disappearing Bus Tour.'"

"It doesn't work that way," I replied. "He has to cut everything into small pieces and swallow it. It takes months."

"Oh." Kevin seemed disappointed. "Well, how about a TV miniseries, then? Or we could set up a hotline, 1-900-EAT-A-BUS, and charge people three bucks a minute to hear him talk about how—"

I didn't catch the rest because my chair was yanked out from under me, sending me crashing to the floor. Rough hands grabbed me by the collar, and I was yanked to my feet by two of Chase's football linemen. Hot breath from their bull nostrils took the curl out of my hair.

"Let him go," muttered Chase.

"Come on, take a punch!" I egged him on. "I'd rather lose all my teeth than owe anything to the likes of you!"

"Don't push your luck, Warren," he warned as he took his seat, followed by his two goons.

I concentrated on Amanda. She was now staring at Chase with *twice* as much admiration and adoration as before. I guess he'd been wearing his very best underwear yesterday. Unbelievable.

To make matters even worse, Mr. Chin was trying to get me to change my topic for the oral presentation.

"I know you're disappointed, Warren," the teacher told me. "But I really don't see that there's enough material available about the man for a whole term assignment."

"I know that," I defended myself. "That's why I wrote Mr. Mactavish a letter. I'll bet he can send me tons of information."

Mr. Chin frowned. "How did you find his address?"

"Oh, I just put Inverness, Scotland, on the envelope," I replied airily. "After all, how many Hamish Mactavishes could there be?"

"Mactavish is one of the most popular names in Scotland!" he exploded. "Hamish Mactavish is like being named Joe Smith over here!"

"Oh." My face fell. "I just figured it was taking him a long time to get back to me because he was so busy, what with eating a bus and all."

The teacher sighed. "There's still time to choose a new topic. I think you'll have no trouble finding someone a lot more admirable than a wild eccentric who's doing something silly."

I leaped to my feet, feeling the hairs on the back of my neck standing on end. "It's not silly," I protested. "Don't you get it? Hamish Mactavish is a total loser. He's fat, he's ugly, he's not too bright—if there's anyone with a good excuse to throw in the towel in life, it's him. But he didn't! He found the one thing he can do that's absolutely unique! Okay, it's a crazy, stupid thing, but it's *his* crazy, stupid thing, and nobody can touch him at it! And in a world where Hamish Mactavish can hit it big, none of us are ever hopeless!"

I sat down amidst the laughter and jeers. Spitballs and erasers bounced off of me. People were whistling inspirational music, and playing imaginary violins. In one short speech, I had cemented my position as the class joke. Even the teacher wore a big grin, although he was trying to hide it.

In fact, the only nonparticipant in this party at my expense was Chase, who sat staring straight forward, his expression inscrutable. Still mad over the Krazy Glue thing, I guess.

▲   ▲   ▲

It was the night before the oral presentations were set to begin. All in all, a pretty ordinary night at our house except that Chase had wrangled the best spot on the couch, so I was crammed into the corner with a lousy view of the TV.

". . . and finally," the news anchor was saying, "the latest word from Inverness, Scotland, is that Hamish Mactavish has given up his bid to eat a bus. According to the forty-one-year-old Mactavish, he was having trouble digesting the tires."

The sportscaster started to make some kind of a wisecrack, but I was already running for the stairs.

"Warren—" my father called.

I burst into my room and slammed the door. I couldn't believe it was all over. Just like that. One minute something special, *historic* was going on, and I was part of it. The next I was nobody again.

I don't know why I felt so betrayed. Hamish Mactavish didn't owe me anything. Who was I to talk? I wouldn't even eat broccoli, let alone seven tons of metal and glass and rubber.

There was knock at my door. "Warren, open up."

It wasn't my folks. It was Chase the Disgrace, probably to rub salt in my wounds.

"Get lost," I snarled.

"I'm really sorry, Warren," Chase said from the hall. "I know how much Hamish What's-his-name meant to you."

"He's a quitter!" I rasped.

"He made an amazing run," Chase amended. "Nobody could have come as close as he did."

It hit me right then: Fighting with my brother got on my nerves, sure. But Chase actually being *nice*—that drove me absolutely insane!

"Leave me alone!" I bellowed. "Go call Amanda! Go be the star of the world!"

Calm down, I told myself. My heart was pounding in my throat. This was 50 percent of my social studies grade, and I was poised to flunk in spectacular style. I had until morning to think up another subject—like Sting, or maybe Harriet Tubman. Then the plan was to get down on my knees, howl at the moon, tear my hair out, and beg, plead, entreat, and cajole Mr. Chin to please, please, *please* have a heart, and give me an extension!

▲　▲　▲

"I knew he couldn't do it," Kevin greeted me in class the next morning.

"Shut up, Kevin," I yawned, bleary-eyed from a sleepless night. "You were ready to send the guy on a coast-to-coast publicity tour!"

"Not anymore," he replied. "His marketability is permanently damaged. I couldn't book him into a grade-school cafeteria, let alone the L.A. Colliseum. You know what our mistake was? The Scotland thing. Why should we go to some foreign country for our superstar? There's plenty of talent right here at home. If we searched the Midwest, I'll bet we could find some farm boy who could eat a combine harvester on national television. Now *that's* American."

Mr. Chin breezed into the room, and I immediately put my plan into action. "Sir? Could I have a word with—"

"Later, Warren," he cut me off. "I want to get started with the oral presentations. Who would like to be first?"

Normally, no one would volunteer, and the teacher would have to pick somebody. But this time there was a hand raised in our social studies class. Most amazing of all, it belonged to Chase the Disgrace. I couldn't believe it. My brother would *never* put his image on the line and be first at something.

"Ah, Chase," the teacher approved. "Go ahead."

As Chase walked to the front of the class, I checked out Amanda. Instead of staring at my brother in nauseating rapture, she was looking over at me! What was going on here?

"Most people think of heroes as winners," Chase read from his notes, "but I'm not convinced that's always true. It's no big deal to pick up a basketball if you're Michael Jordan, or to do something you know you're going to be great at. What's a lot harder is to try something even when the odds are stacked up against you. Sometimes failing is more admirable than succeeding. . . ."

It all clicked into place in a moment of exquisite agony—Chase's sudden kindness last night, his volunteering to go first, Amanda watching me, not him. After a lifetime of beating, outperforming, and besting me in every imaginable way, Chase was delivering the final *ultimate* insult. He had figured out a way to do his oral presentation on Hamish

Mactavish when I couldn't. He was even better than me at *being* me!

The dam burst, and white-hot blinding rage flooded my brain. "*Why you double-crossing—*" I leaped out of my chair, and made a run at my brother, with every intention of leaving this class an only child.

"Warren!" Mr. Chin stopped me a scant six inches from Chase's throat. "Have you lost your mind?" He held me by the shoulders, his face flushed, but not half as red as mine must have been.

"You're the lowest of the low!" I seethed at Chase. "You're the slime trail of the mutant parasites that crawl around the sludge of the toxic waste dump!"

"Warren, go to the principal's office!" ordered the teacher.

Chase stepped in. "Please, Mr. Chin, let him stay. I want him to hear this." He returned to his notes, and continued his presentation. "The person I picked isn't always successful, but he's heroic because he never gives up when a lot of us would. When *I* definitely would. That person is my brother Warren."

There are times in this life when you feel like the biggest total moron in the galaxy, but you just have to stand there and take it, because anything you say will only make things twenty times worse. My jaw was hanging around my knees, as Chase went on about my strength of character and my resilience; how others fell to pieces when the cards didn't come up aces, while I was always ready to do my best with the two of clubs.

When he finished, all eyes in the class were on me. And for the first time ever, I couldn't think of a single rotten thing to say to Chase the Disgrace.

"This doesn't mean I like you," I managed finally.

He stuck out his jaw. "You either."

"Of course, you're not such a bad guy," I added quickly.

"We're brothers," he replied with a grin. "We've got to support each other."

I pounced on this. "Switch rooms with me?"

"In your dreams!" laughed Chase.

"Pinhead."

"Doofus."

"Idiot."

"Look who's talking—"

Well, at least I was his hero. That was a start. ❧

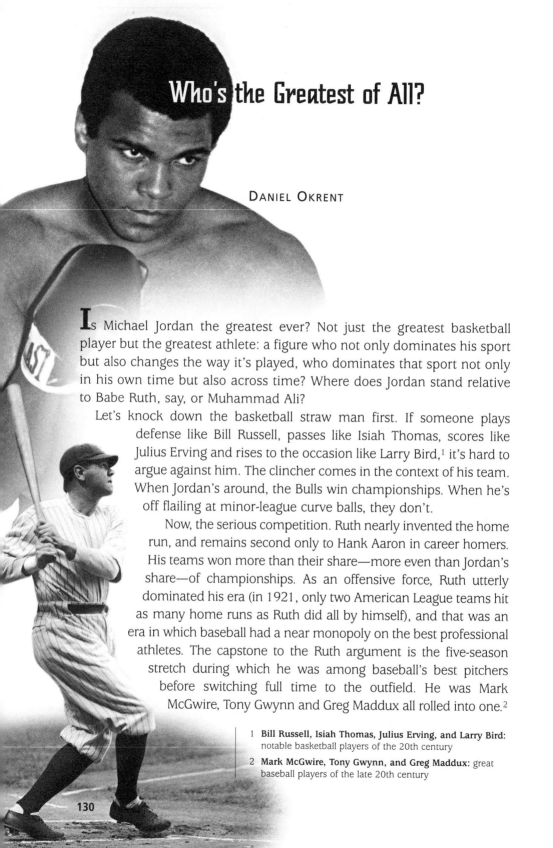

Who's the Greatest of All?

DANIEL OKRENT

Is Michael Jordan the greatest ever? Not just the greatest basketball player but the greatest athlete: a figure who not only dominates his sport but also changes the way it's played, who dominates that sport not only in his own time but also across time? Where does Jordan stand relative to Babe Ruth, say, or Muhammad Ali?

Let's knock down the basketball straw man first. If someone plays defense like Bill Russell, passes like Isiah Thomas, scores like Julius Erving and rises to the occasion like Larry Bird,[1] it's hard to argue against him. The clincher comes in the context of his team. When Jordan's around, the Bulls win championships. When he's off flailing at minor-league curve balls, they don't.

Now, the serious competition. Ruth nearly invented the home run, and remains second only to Hank Aaron in career homers. His teams won more than their share—more even than Jordan's share—of championships. As an offensive force, Ruth utterly dominated his era (in 1921, only two American League teams hit as many home runs as Ruth did all by himself), and that was an era in which baseball had a near monopoly on the best professional athletes. The capstone to the Ruth argument is the five-season stretch during which he was among baseball's best pitchers before switching full time to the outfield. He was Mark McGwire, Tony Gwynn and Greg Maddux all rolled into one.[2]

---

1 **Bill Russell, Isiah Thomas, Julius Erving, and Larry Bird:** notable basketball players of the 20th century

2 **Mark McGwire, Tony Gwynn, and Greg Maddux:** great baseball players of the late 20th century

But Ruth's accomplishments are diminished by one brutal fact: he didn't play against black athletes. One-tenth of the population, and surely a far larger proportion of those motivated to succeed in athletics, never had a chance to test Ruth. I hate to admit it, but it may be that the Babe was more George Mikan[3] than Michael Jordan.

Ali? Among those in individual sports, his record is without peer, as was his combination of talents: size, speed, power, guile and the colossal heart that vanquished the great Joe Frazier. But Ali suffers from the converse of the Ruth argument: by the time Ali came along, the best athletes had been siphoned off[4] by team sports. Ali was a giant, but most of his opponents were relative dwarfs.

Jim Brown?[5] Just nine seasons, offense only. Jim Thorpe?[6] More legend than accomplishment. Jack Nicklaus? Sorry, but golfers, like tennis players and decathletes, don't have to suffer flying elbows, inside sliders or other lethal moving objects. Hockey has until recently attracted only athletes from colder regions. There has simply never been an athletic accomplishment on the scale of Jordan's in the U.S.

But that national qualifier is critical. If you're looking for the best in the world, you would have to pick someone who dominated a sport played by more than 200 million people, most from countries where no other game matters enough to draw down the talent pool; an athlete who at 17 led his team to the first of his unprecedented three world championships, who in a sport accustomed to the 1-0 shutout scored an astonishing 1,281 goals. For my money, if you have to pick the one best athlete of all time, it's Brazil's nonpareil[7] Pelé, the Michael Jordan of soccer. ∞

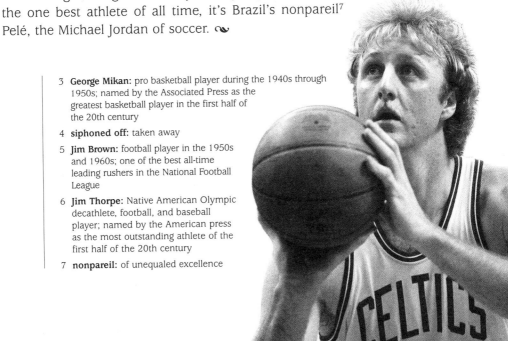

3 **George Mikan:** pro basketball player during the 1940s through 1950s; named by the Associated Press as the greatest basketball player in the first half of the 20th century

4 **siphoned off:** taken away

5 **Jim Brown:** football player in the 1950s and 1960s; one of the best all-time leading rushers in the National Football League

6 **Jim Thorpe:** Native American Olympic decathlete, football, and baseball player; named by the American press as the most outstanding athlete of the first half of the 20th century

7 **nonpareil:** of unequaled excellence

Dr. Martin Luther King, Jr.

D AVID D INKINS

*David Dinkins, who would later become the mayor of
New York City, delivered this speech several days after
Dr. King was assassinated.*

Martin Luther King is dead now, and we, the mourners and losers, are left with his dreams—with decisions to make. He is dead now, and there are no words we can say for him, for he said his own. He is dead now, and any eulogy[1] must be for us, the living.

Martin Luther King is dead now, so for him there is no tomorrow on this earth. But for us there are tomorrows and tomorrows. He painted a picture of what our tomorrows could be in his dream of America. This past weekend painted a picture of how that dream could become a nightmare should we lose sight of his principles.

Martin Luther King is dead now, but he left a legacy.[2] He planted in all of us, black and white, the seeds of love of justice, of decency, of honor, and we must not fail to have these seeds bear fruit.

Martin Luther King is dead now, and there is only time for action. The time for debate, the time for blame, the time for accusation is over. Ours is a clear call to action. We must not only dedicate ourselves to great principles, but we must apply those principles to our lives.

Martin Luther King is dead now, and he is because he dared believe in nonviolence in a world of violence. Because he dared believe in peace in

---

1 **eulogy:** commendation or praise usually given at a funeral

2 **legacy:** a gift given to future generations

a world of conflict. He is dead now because he challenged all of us to believe in his dream.

Martin Luther King is dead now, and we cannot allow the substance of his dream to turn into the ashes of defeat. If we are to build a tribute to what he stood for, we must, each of us, stand for the same things.

Martin Luther King is dead now, and I ask each of you, the living, to join him and me, to go from this room and keep the dream alive. We must now commit ourselves, we must now work, we must now define what kind of America we are going to have—for unless we make his dream a reality we will not have an America about which to decide.

Martin Luther King is dead now—but he lives. ∾

Visible Ink

NIKKI GIOVANNI

PART OF GROWING   1991   Brenda Joysmith

In many respects Samson[1] was a vain . . . if not actually silly . . . man . . . certainly he knew the source of his great strength . . . though he mistakenly thought it was his hair . . . and not the God . . . who gave it to him

Achilles'[2] strength was thought to be the water . . . he was dipped in . . . not the faith of his mother . . . who took him to the river

Women count on their looks . . . adolescents their youth . . . yet we all look for a champion . . . we all believe in some sort of magic . . . whether it is the state lottery or a longshot at the races . . . we turn to some sort of otherness . . . to change our luck

Superman fell in love . . . with Lois and was willing . . . to give up his great powers for her . . . in order to marry Wallis Simpson, Edward . . . gave up the throne of England[3] . . . One wonders not if the right thing was done . . . but if what was given . . . was worth what was taken . . . the very nature of sacrifice says: There Is No Parity[4] . . . One does what one must in order to be a whole . . . complete . . . human

---

1 **Samson:** Biblical strong man who lost his strength after his hair was cut

2 **Achilles:** Greek mythological hero who, as a child, was dipped in the river Styx by his goddess mother in an attempt to protect his body from wounds

3 **Edward:** British king (Edward VIII) who married an American socialite, thus giving up the throne before completing his first year in that position

4 **Parity:** equality

And then there is that cry . . . that cry of Samson who recognized his own foolishness . . . that cry of Superman who finally realized he was . . . indeed . . . more than mortal man . . . and must face his destiny . . . we don't know the last thoughts of Malcolm X . . . or Martin Luther King, Jr., we can't know the deeper thought of the Brown family as they sent little Linda off to school[5] . . . we might guess that Emmett Till's mother wishes she could take her boy back[6] . . . as we might understand Afeni Shakur begging her son: Honey, wake up and let's go home[7] . . . The greatest heroes probably have no idea . . . how heroic they are

Most people think of heroes as saving children from flaming buildings or pulling housewives from automobile wrecks . . . But it is . . . indeed . . . heroic to pay one's bills at the end of the month . . . to go to church on Sundays and sing in the choir . . . to referee a softball game or teach some child how to make apple cobbler

The heroes of our time do the ordinary things that must be done . . . whether we are applauded or not . . . Most of us are good people . . . Most of us want to do the right things . . . We want to be loving to our families . . . caring for our elderly . . . wise for our young . . . We want to be a hero in our own eyes . . . We celebrate the true Champions of the 20th Century . . . because they went one step further

They willingly made a sacrifice of time . . . fortune . . . and in some cases their lives . . . to make life on the planet a more meaningful experience . . . That they are African American can come as no surprise . . . The African American has continually stepped up when the right . . . the good . . . the proper . . . needed to be counted

The Champions of the 20th Century have put their lives . . . their hopes . . . their best wishes . . . on the line so that future generations will sing the praises of our people . . . who continue to know . . . where the true strength comes from ∾

5 **Linda Brown:** black elementary student in Kansas whose parents fought for school integration in 1954; their battle reached the Supreme Court

6 **Emmett Till:** a Chicago boy who was killed in 1955 by white men in a racially motivated incident

7 **Afeni Shakur:** mother of Tupac Shakur, a black activist/musician. In 1996, Tupac Shakur was shot four times and died six days later.

The Woodcutter's Story

NANCY SCHIMMEL

Once upon a time there lived a king and a queen who had three sons. When the sons were grown, the king called them together and said, "The time will come when I will no longer wish to be king, and one of you will rule in my stead.[1] Therefore, you must go out, each in turn, to learn about the world. I will give my kingdom to the one who first rescues a woman from mortal danger." He was a traditional sort of king. "Since you are my first-born son," he said to the eldest, "you will have the first chance."

So the eldest prince mounted his fine horse and rode off to seek his fortune, feeling as brave and confident as he looked. He knew exactly what would happen. He would rescue no less than a princess and from something fierce and interesting, like a dragon.

He rode along and rode along, and he came to an old woman standing by the road, holding a frayed rope attached to a sleek and restless nannygoat. "O prince!" called the old woman, immediately recognizing his station in life, "O prince, please milk my goat, for I cannot milk her."

"Nor can I," said the prince, "for I am a prince, and I was not taught to do such things." The prince rode on and rode on, and he came to a young woman holding a wriggling, yowling baby.

"O prince!" she called, "please feed my baby, for he is hungry as a horse, and I cannot feed him."

"A horse I could feed," replied the prince, "but not a baby, for I am a man, and I was not taught to do such things." The prince rode on and rode on, and he came to an old man standing by the road, holding a large and shiny ax.

1 **stead:** place or position

"O prince!" called the old man, "please take my ax, for I can no longer swing it. I am a woodcutter for the king, and my house and my tools are yours if you would serve him in my stead."

"I would serve your king, old man," said the prince, "but I cannot stay here in the woods with you. I must learn about the world and rescue some endangered princess. My future and my country's future depend on it."

So the eldest prince rode on. Soon he came to a castle, where he put himself in service to a king. He became a valiant knight, fought mighty battles, and killed many men, but somehow he never managed to rescue a princess, or indeed any woman, from mortal danger.

The second prince, still at home, was eager for his chance at the kingdom, but he was puzzled, for he knew that his eldest brother had won fame as a knight yet had failed to win the kingdom. When he asked his father's advice on the matter, the king replied, "There's more to kingship than battles."

Well, the second prince rode out on his fine horse, intending to rescue a princess or at least a fine lady. He took the same road his brother had taken and gave the same answers to the old woman with the goat, the young woman with the baby, and the old man with the ax. But when he arrived at the castle, he remembered his father's advice and put himself in service to the king as a courtier.[2] He learned much of fine manners and smooth speech and something of statecraft and the work of kings. Indeed, he met several princesses and many fine ladies, but not one of them needed rescuing from anything more threatening than boredom.

The last remaining prince was still at home, and being the youngest, he was not so eager to go out into the world. But he knew his father was depending on him to go and seek his fortune, so he curried[3] and fed his horse and asked his father's advice. "Ruling a country requires more than brave deeds and fine manners," said the king. Now, this prince thought to ask his mother's advice as well. "You never know where your fortune might lie," said the queen, "but it helps to look in your own heart."

So the youngest prince rode out on his fine horse, intending to rescue a princess or a fine lady or at least a beautiful maiden. He took the same road his brothers had taken, but when he got out of sight of the castle, he got off his horse and walked awhile, the better to say goodbye to the

2 **courtier:** attendant in a royal court

3 **curried:** combed; cleaned

fields and flowers of home. Then he remounted and rode along and rode along, until he came to the old woman with the goat. When she asked him to milk her goat, the prince said, "As I am a prince, no one ever thought to teach me to milk a goat. However, if you will tell me what to do, I will try."

"Certainly," she said. So the youngest prince dismounted, and under the woman's patient direction he finally managed to milk the fidgety goat. "Thank you," said the old woman, taking the pail of foamy milk. "Now that you can milk the goat, you may have her."

"Whatever would I do with a goat?" cried the prince. But there was no reply, for the old woman had disappeared. The goat looked at the prince expectantly. "Oh, all right," muttered the prince. He took the rope in his hand and mounted his horse. He rode on and rode on, and he came to the young woman with the bawling baby.

"O prince!" she called, "please feed my baby, for I cannot feed him."

"Well," said the prince, glancing sidelong at the goat, "I do seem to have this goat, and I've learned to milk her, but I've never fed a baby."

"There's nothing to it," said the woman. So the prince dismounted and milked the goat, and he and the woman fed the baby. "Now you must burp him," said the woman.

"What?" asked the prince.

"Burp him," said the woman. "Hold him against your shoulder, like so, and pat his back, like this." She spread a napkin on the prince's princely raiment[4] and handed him the baby. "Now that you can feed the baby," she said, "you may have him."

"I can't take this baby," shouted the prince, but it was to no avail, for the young woman had disappeared. The prince sighed, tucked the fat, gurgling baby under his arm, tied the goat's frayed rope to his tastefully bejeweled saddle, and clambered back onto his horse. He rode on and rode on, and he came to the old man with the large and shiny ax. The prince closed his eyes.

"O prince!" called the old man. The prince sighed again and opened his eyes. "O prince, please take my ax, for I can no longer swing it. I am woodcutter for the king, and my house and my tools are yours if you would serve him in my stead."

The prince furrowed his brow. "I would serve your king," he said, "but this seems to be turning out all wrong. I thought I was supposed to learn

4 **raiment:** garment

to be a king and rescue a princess, but instead I seem to have this baby and this goat. I suppose I could use a house and a job as well . . ." The prince scratched his head. "What am I supposed to do?" The old man made no reply but simply offered a gnarled finger to the baby. The prince's horse shifted its weight, the goat bleated, the baby crooned, and off in the woods a bird sang. The prince remembered his mother's words, looked into his heart, and smiled. "I think I will stay here," he said, "and learn to be a woodcutter."

The prince settled easily into his new life. The old woodcutter loved his trade and taught the prince everything he knew. They both had a way with babies, and as the baby grew into a boy, they both delighted in teaching him the names of the woodland flowers and creatures. The boy delighted in everything.

Most of the time the prince was content to be cutting the sweet-smelling wood, keeping house with the old man and the boy, and visiting with the common folk of the nearby farms. His neighbors didn't even think of him as a prince anymore. "The new woodcutter," they called him. Still, he was a prince, and he worried because he wasn't learning about battles or statecraft. He was learning to deal diplomatically with mischievous boys and goats and learning some of the stories the old woodcutter told, but mostly he was learning about hard work and the people who did it.

And then sometimes he would think about his father, the king, waiting patiently for his youngest son to rescue a woman from mortal danger and return to rule the kingdom. The nearest princess was in the castle, and the prince never even drove the wagon there to deliver the wood, for that was still the old man's job. Besides, no one had ever seen a dragon in the neighborhood. A wolf or two, perhaps, but that was no help, for all the beautiful maidens 'round about were sturdy farmhands, and no sensible wolf would have dared attack one of them.

One day as the prince sat musing on his unprincely life, the boy ran into the cottage and pulled himself up on the prince's lap. "You know that girl who comes to visit her grandmother in the house down the path?"

"Mmm," said the prince, gazing into the middle distance.

"Well," continued the boy, "her mother made her a red cape with a red hood, and now all the kids are calling her Little Red Riding Hood. Isn't that funny?"

"That's nice," said the prince, but he wasn't listening. He was thinking that he would have to send word to his father that he would never rescue anyone from anything in this peaceful neighborhood. "You run along and play," he said to the boy, giving him a hug and setting him down. "I'll be along in a bit. I'm thinking about something important." The prince sat for a while longer, frowning, then shrugged his shoulders, got up, and went outside. The boy and the old woodcutter were playing knight and horse. The new woodcutter gazed at them fondly for a moment, then picked up his ax and said, "I'm going to the woods. I'll be back in a while."

It is on the shady path that we will take our leave of the youngest prince. At first he walks slowly, scuffling at leaves, but soon he is whistling, and as he turns the bend that will take him from this story into another one, a ray of sunlight catches his ax, and it seems to wink at us. ❧

Responding to Cluster Four

Thinking Skill SYNTHESIZING

1. Each of the other clusters in this book is introduced by a question that is meant to help readers focus their thinking about the selections. What do you think the question for Cluster Four should be?

2. How do you think the selections in this cluster should be taught? Demonstrate your ideas by joining with your classmates to
   - create discussion questions
   - lead discussions about the selections
   - develop vocabulary activities
   - prepare a cluster quiz

Reflecting on *To Be a Hero*

Essential Question WHO CAN BE A HERO?

Reflecting on this book as a whole provides an opportunity for independent learning and the application of the critical thinking skill synthesis. *Synthesizing* means examining all the things you have learned from this book and combining them to form a richer and more meaningful view of heroism.

There are many ways to demonstrate what you know about heroism. Here are some possibilities. Your teacher may provide others.

1. Reread the essay at the beginning of this book, "Boy, Do We Ever Need a Hero." Prepare a debate for the classroom by supporting or opposing this statement, "We have no heroes today."

2. Individually or in small groups, develop an independent project that demonstrates what you have learned about heroes. For example, you might choose a category of heroes and create a visual montage of this type of hero throughout history. Or you might wish to create an imaginary hero in a fairy tale or fable. Other options might include a music video, poem, performance, or drama.

AUTHOR BIOGRAPHIES

DAVE BARRY Dave Barry believes that he'll never be funnier than dogs or the U.S. government, and his writings often center on exploding or flaming items, stupid dogs, or amusing political incidents. A natural comedian, Barry's writing career began with short humor pieces that he wrote for his high school newspaper. Today his column is published in over 500 newspapers nationwide. Barry has written 23 books and won numerous awards, including the Pulitzer Prize for his 1988 book, *Commentary*. His non-literary endeavors have included the CBS sitcom "Dave's World," based on two of his books, and playing lead guitarist in the rock band Rock Bottom Remainders, made up entirely of authors—including Stephen King and Amy Tan. Barry lives with his wife and children in Miami, Florida.

CHRISTY BROWN Born in Dublin, Ireland, Christy Brown was one of thirteen surviving children of hard-working parents. Afflicted with cerebral palsy, he was considered mentally disabled for much of his childhood. His mother, however, was determined to help develop his skills from early on. When he famously grabbed a piece of chalk from his sister with his left foot, the only part of his body over which he had control, Christy Brown's keen and thirsty mind was evident to those around him. Using that left foot, Brown learned to paint and then to write. The autobiography that resulted was aptly titled *My Left Foot*. This was eventually expanded into the novel, *Down All the Days*, which became an international bestseller and was translated into fourteen languages. After the success of his first book, Christy went on to write other novels and a number of poetry collections. In 1989 Jim Sheridan created the film *My Left Foot*, starring Daniel Day Lewis as Christy Brown.

JOSEPH BRUCHAC A well-known storyteller from upstate New York, Joseph Bruchac draws heavily from his Abenaki Indian ancestry in his writing. Working with family members on projects to preserve Abenaki culture, language, and traditional skills, Bruchac tells traditional Native American stories that advise people how to respect the Earth and behave towards others. After earning a BA from Cornell University, an MA from Syracuse University, and a PhD from the Union Institute, Bruchac continued his writing and teaching. In 1971 he helped found the Greenfield Review Press, publisher of multicultural books and recordings. He has also edited several highly praised anthologies of contemporary poetry and fiction.

REBECCA CHRISTIAN A resident of Des Moines, Iowa, Rebecca Christian is involved with the history and arts of the Midwest. She is a correspondent for the *Des Moines Register* and *Midwest Living* as well as a veteran of the Iowa Arts Council's Artists in Schools and Communities program. A writer, humorist, public radio contributor and playwright, Christian tells stories with startling wit and humanity. Her comic drama about Iowa women, *Wish Me Pretty, Wish Me Strong*, tells a potent story through the eyes of women in history. It won an Iowa Humanities Board Award. She also wrote the play *First Lady Lou* about the life and times of Lou Hoover, the wife of President Herbert Hoover.

DAVID DINKINS As the first African American mayor of New York City, David Dinkins focused on crime and the problems of racial inequality. Elected mayor in 1989, Dinkins inherited a budget deficit of $500 million and one quarter of the city's population living in poverty. He initiated a program called "Safe Streets, Safe City: Cops and Kids," concentrating on the issues of drug abuse prevention, AIDS, housing, and education. After losing the 1993 mayoral race to Rudy Giuliani, Dinkins continued his criticism of the criminal justice system and was arrested while protesting the shooting of Amadou Diallo, an unarmed immigrant shot by NYPD police officers. Dinkins is currently a professor at Columbia University School of International and Public Affairs. He also hosts a public affairs radio program, "Dialogues with Dinkins."

IAN FRAZIER According to Ian Frazier, "words are charms," and his writing often conveys the deep impact of these charms. Frazier grew up in Ohio and graduated from Harvard University in 1977. At Harvard he wrote for the *Lampoon*, a humorous student newspaper. He then wrote for *The New Yorker* before branching off to write several best-selling novels, including *On the Rez, Great Plains, Coyote v. Acme*, and *Dating Your Mom*. In *Great Plains*, Frazier, describing himself as a refugee from New York, drives to Montana to research the area. He conveys the history, topography, and people of the area, and gives a convincing argument against any further exploitation of this great land. Frazier writing informs the reader of the tremendous impact the Native American culture has had on the United States.

NICHOLAS GAGE Born Nikos Gatzoyiannis in 1939 in a remote Greek village below the Albanian border, Gage's writing draws extensively from his childhood in Greece and his later immigrant experience in America. As a young boy in Greece, Nikos was without his father, who worked in Massachusetts to support the family. Nikos did not meet his father until he and his sisters were found in a refugee camp during WWII and shipped to Massachusetts. Gage's early personal essays won him a scholarship to Boston University. In college, he won the Hearst Award for best college journalist in the U.S. and went on to study at the Columbia Graduate School of Journalism. Later, as a reporter for the *New York Times*, Gage was sent to Athens as a foreign correspondent for the Middle East. After several years in Athens, he left the *Times* to devote himself to investigating and writing the story of his mother's life and death. Titled *Eleni*, the book was published in 1983 to much acclaim. Gage has since written several books about growing up in Greece, Greek history and culture, and other related subjects.

NIKKI GIOVANNI Born Yolande Cornelia Giovanni, Jr., in Knoxville, Tennessee, Nikki Giovanni is considered a leader in the black poetry movement. After graduating from Fisk University with a history degree, Giovanni went on to attend the University of Pennsylvania School of Social Work and the Columbia University School of Fine Arts. Believing that change is necessary for growth, Giovanni's poetry is renowned for it's call of urgency for black people to realize their identities and understand white-controlled culture. Her poetry collection *Black Feeling, Black Talk/ Black Judgment* captures the militant attitude of the civil rights and black arts movements of the early 1960s. Her work has been honored with a number of NAACP Image Awards as well as the Langston Hughes Medal for Outstanding Poetry. Giovanni prides herself on being "a Black American, a daughter, a mother, and a professor of English."

ROBERT HAYDEN Due to impaired vision, Robert Hayden could not participate in sports as a boy, so he absorbed himself in reading. Born Asa Bundy Sheffey in Detroit in 1913, his parents divorced when he was young. He was raised by foster parents William and Sue Hayden. His was an emotionally tumultuous childhood, though Hayden remained in contact with each of his biological parents while growing up. He graduated from Fisk University in Tennessee and went on to study with the poet W. H. Auden while earning his master's degree at the University of Michigan. Hayden's meticulously crafted and thoughtful poetry explores human dilemmas in the context of race and African American history. Throughout most of his adult life Hayden was a college professor, also winning numerous awards for his poetry. In 1976 he was appointed consultant to the Library of Congress, the first African American to hold this position.

KRISTIN HUNTER As an African American novelist, Kristin Hunter is committed to telling the truth, not just the agony and happiness of the black woman. She marvels at the ways African Americans seem to bend, but not break, in order to survive. Hunter's novel *Kinfolks* was nominated for the National Book Award, and like her other works, examines black life and racial relations in the U.S. Over the years, Hunter has worked as an elementary school teacher, an advertising copywriter, a TV scriptwriter, and finally as professor of creative writing at the University of Pennsylvania. Hunter has published over ten works of fiction for both children and adults and currently lives in New Jersey.

GORDON KORMAN Gordon Korman wrote his first story at the age of twelve as an assignment for school. This story was eventually expanded into a book and published by Scholastic. At last count, Korman had over 55 books to his credit. He is the author of several young-adult humor and adventure series, four of which were ALA Best Books for Young Adults. Originally from Montreal, Canada, Korman currently lives in New York City, but also spends time in Toronto and Florida with his wife and three children. "Keep on laughing" is his winning philosophy.

JOANNA HALPERT KRAUS Joanna Kraus has written over fourteen published and internationally produced plays, her most popular being *Ice Wolf*. This drama set in Alaska was first produced off Broadway and was the winner of the 1996 Distinguished Play Award. Kraus is the Professor Emeritus of Theater and former graduate coordinator of interdisciplinary arts at the State University of New York College at Brockport. Other popular plays by Kraus include *Remember My Name, Ms. Courageous, Tall Boy's Journey*, and *Angel in the Night*.

DANIEL OKRENT Daniel Okrent has a varied and impressive resume as a writer and editor. After graduating from the University of Michigan in 1969, Okrent enjoyed editorial stints at several distinguished publishing houses before becoming a columnist for *Esquire* magazine in 1985, where he was twice awarded the National Magazine Award for General Excellence. Okrent then became the founding editor of *New England* magazine, after which he undertook the managing editor position at *Life* magazine, followed by an editor-at-large post with *Time*. He has enjoyed over 25 years in the magazine and book publishing industry and became the first public editor for *The New York Times* in 2003, a position he held for two years. Okrent has also written several books, including *Great Fortune: The Epic of Rockefeller Center*, which appeared in 2003. Okrent is also an avid baseball fan.

GARY PAULSEN At the age of fourteen, Gary Paulsen ran away from an unhappy home to travel with a circus. This experience spurred an enduring sense of adventure, and was the first of many varied endeavors—from engineer, to farmer, construction worker, ranch hand, truck driver, and sailor. He has even competed in the Iditarod Trail Sled Dog Race, a grueling 1,150-mile race held yearly in Alaska. Many of Paulsen's life experiences are reflected in the more than 175 books he has written. His success as a writer stems from his ability to tap into the human spirit in a way that encourages the reader to observe and care about the world. His novels *Hatchet, Dogsong*, and *The Winter Room* were given the Newbery Award. Paulsen lives with his wife Ruth, an artist who has illustrated several of his books.

ROGER ROSENBLATT As a journalist, author, playwright, and teacher, Roger Rosenblatt has won numerous awards, including the 1983 Robert F. Kennedy Book Prize for *Children of War*. Rosenblatt has presented his essays for the PBS television program "NewsHour," and for a number of magazines, including *Time, Vanity Fair*, and *Esquire*. He has been a columnist and editor-at-large for *Life* magazine, and was editor of *US News and World Report*. Rosenblatt earned a Ph.D. from Harvard University. He teaches literary essay writing at the University of Long Island's Southampton College. Rosenblatt is also the author of ten books, including the national bestseller *Rules for Aging*.

NANCY SCHIMMEL Storytelling is in Nancy Schimmel's blood. She grew up listening to her father's captivating tales of sailing on a ship that was forced to carry freight during WWI. She also enjoyed the enchanting songs her mother sang. She got her start telling stories while a camp counselor, and then continued her storytelling at local fairs while working as a librarian. From 1977 to 1981, Schimmel crisscrossed the country in a big white van dubbed "Moby Jane" with a group of other storytellers. In her first book, *Just Enough to Make a Story*, Schimmel wrote about her experiences teaching storytelling courses to adults in libraries. She now tells stories all over the U.S. and abroad in schools, hospitals, libraries, festivals, and countless other settings. In addition to her book, Nancy has several published stories, recordings, and articles.

ROSEMARY SUTCLIFF Stills Disease, a form of juvenile arthritis, kept young Rosemary Sutcliff under her mother's watchful eye in Surrey, England. Her home schooling included traditional Celtic, Norse, and Saxon myths and legends, read to her by her mother. Sutcliff did not learn to read until she was nine years old. She entered the Bideford Art School in 1934, finishing the General Art Course in three years. In 1946 she began writing for publication the stories she had learned as a child. She soon received a commission to create a children's version of the legend of Robin Hood. Sutcliff loved immersing herself in an era, and enjoyed letting history guide the plot development. In 1992, shortly before her death, Sutcliff was made a CBE (Commander of the British Empire) for her contributions to British literature.

PHIL TAYLOR An avid sports fan, Phil Taylor chooses basketball as his favorite game to play as well as write about. He believes the 1986 World Series was his most memorable moment in sports history. A native of Queens New York, Taylor received his BA from Amherst College in 1982 and an MA from Stanford in 1983. He worked as a sports writer and columnist for the *San Jose Mercury News* and the *Miami Herald* before joining the staff of *Sports Illustrated* in 1990. Phil lives in northern California with his wife and three children.

BRIAN M. THOMSEN With more than 25 years of publishing experience, Brian M. Thomsen has published over 30 short stories and numerous fiction and nonfiction anthologies. In addition, he has written two novels and was nominated for a Hugo Award. Thomsen served as a World Fantasy Award judge and lives in Brooklyn with his wife.

ALISOUN WITTING Alisoun Witting worked as a reporter and photographer for the *Castine Patriot* in Maine. Her *Treasury of Greek Mythology* is a comprehensive collection of Greek myths.

JANE YOLEN Jane Yolen has been called "America's Hans Christian Anderson," for her immensely popular children's fantasy books. Yolen's great-grandfather was a teller of tales in his Finno-Russian village. In addition, her parents also followed this creative tradition. Her mother wrote short stories and her father was a journalist. After graduating from Smith College, where she wrote poetry and worked on the school paper, Yolen moved to New York City to become an editor. She wrote stories and poems on her lunch breaks and over the weekends. Her first book, *Pirates in Petticoats*, was published when she was 23, and she has since published over 200 books for children and adults. Her book *Owl Moon* won the Caldecott Medal, and Yolen has become one of the acknowledged masters of fantasy writing.

ADDITIONAL READING

The Adventures of Blue Avenger, Norma Howe. What does a normal 16-year-old boy who becomes the hero of his own comic strip, who falls in love with a girl named Omaha Nebraska Brown, and who invents a recipe for perfect dripless lemon meringue pie have to do with the 16th-century heretic Giordano Bruno and ending the plague of handgun violence in America? Find out! ©2000

The Aeneid, Virgil. The wanderings of hero Aeneas after the Trojan War, which eventually lead to the founding of Rome. ©1961

After the Dancing Days, Margaret I. Rostkowski. A forbidden friendship with a badly disfigured soldier in the aftermath of World War I forces 13-year-old Annie to redefine the word "hero." ©1988

Baree, the Story of a Wolf-Dog (originally published as *Baree, Son of Kazan*), James Oliver Curwood. Accidentally separated from his parents as a pup, Baree learns to fend for himself. Finally, he finds his home with humans, the story culminating in a breathtaking act of heroism on his part. ©1990

Blackwater, Eve Bunting. Brodie Lynch was ready for a perfect summer along the Blackwater River. That was before everything changed forever. When a harmless prank goes too far, the unthinkable happens. Brodie's lies make him a hero, but his guilt tears at him like the current of the Blackwater itself. ©2000

Born to Fly: The Heroic Story of Downed U.S. Navy Pilot Lt. Shane Osborn, Shane Osborn with Malcolm McConnell. The suspenseful story of Osborn's mid-air collision with a Chinese fighter pilot and the heroic emergency landing at a Chinese military base on April 1, 2001. ©2001

The Boys from St. Petri, Bjarne Reuter. In 1942, a group of young men begin a series of increasingly dangerous protests against the German invasion of their Danish homeland. ©1996

The Chief, Robert Lipsyte. A teenaged boxer and his police sergeant mentor need a hero to help them realize their dreams. ©1995

A Different Kind of Hero, Ann R. Blakeslee. In 1881 12-year-old Renny, who resists his father's efforts to turn him into a rough, tough, brawling boy, earns the disapproval of the entire mining camp when he befriends a newly arrived Chinese boy. ©1997

Ender's Game, Orson Scott Card. Aliens have attacked Earth twice and nearly destroyed the human species. To avoid this happening again, the world government begins breeding military geniuses, one of whom is Ender Wiggin. ©1994

Flags of Our Fathers: Heroes of Iwo Jima, James Bradley with Ron Powers, adapted by Michael French. The story of the six young men who came together at one moment during America's most heroic battle to be immortalized by an Associated Press photographer as they hoisted the American flag over Iwo Jima in World War II. ©2001

Flight of the Dragon Kyn, Susan Fletcher. Kara's ability to call down birds attracts the attention of the king, who wants her to try her talent to call down dragons so he can slay them and be a hero. Prequel to *Dragon's Milk.* ©1993

Grace, Jill Paton Walsh. After helping her father rescue the survivors of a shipwreck on the coast of England in 1838, Grace Darling finds her quiet life crumbling around her as she is unwillingly fashioned into a national hero. ©1994

The Hero, Ron Woods. Despite his father's rules and his own fear of the water, 14-year-old Jamie joins his older cousin in taking the raft they made out onto the river, where a tragic accident leads Jamie to make the most difficult decision of his life. ©2002

Hero, Susan L. Rottman. After years of abuse from his mother and neglect from his distant father, Sean Parker is sent to do community service at a farm owned by an old man who teaches Sean that he can take control of his own life. ©1997

The Hero and the Crown, Robin McKinley. Fighting the dragon made girl-warrior Aerin a legend for all time and a true hero who would wield the power of the blue sword. Sequel to *The Blue Sword.* ©1987

Heroes: A Novel, Robert Cormier. Francis is back from World War II, tragically disfigured by a grenade that removed most of his face. Having returned home he has a mission—to kill the childhood hero who destroyed his life. ©2000

Jubilee Journey, Carolyn Meyer. Emily Rose Chantier, the bi-racial 13-year-old great-granddaughter of Rose Lee Jefferson, is invited to Dillon, Texas, to celebrate Juneteenth and to learn about her roots. Sequel to *White Lilacs.* ©1997

The King's Shadow, Elizabeth Alder. Unable to speak, Evyn, a young Welsh serf, is taught to read and write. He becomes the personal companion to the future king of England and chronicles all of their adventures. IRA Children's Book Award. ©1997

The Last Book in the Universe, Rodman Philbrick. Spaz is a young hero who lives in a dangerous future and embarks on a quest to break through the boundaries of the terrifying world he lives in. ©2001

The Last Mission, Harry Mazer. In 1944, 15-year-old Jack dreams of being a hero. Using a false I.D., he lies his way into the U.S. Air Force. ©1981

A Long Way Home, Nancy Graff. After moving to his mother's small hometown in Vermont, 12-year-old Riley must reconsider his feelings about war and heroes when he meets a man who refused to fight in Vietnam and makes a discovery about one of his own relatives. ©2001

The Losers' Club, John Lekich. Alex Sherwood would like to blend in and keep a low profile in his local high school. His plan is thwarted when he inadvertently becomes hero to a group of so-called losers. ©2002

Martyrs' Crossing, Amy Wilentz. A stunning story of love, fear, divided loyalties, ruined friendships, and personal sacrifice set against a backdrop of raging war in the Holy Land. Ballantine Reader's Circle Edition. ©2001

My Brother Sam Is Dead, James Lincoln Collier & Christopher Collier. Tim is torn between his brother's patriotism and his father's Tory sympathies. NCTE, Newbery Honor. ©1985

On Heroes and the Heroic: In Search of Good Deeds, Roger Rosen & Patra McSharry Sevastiades, eds. Photographs, nonfiction essays, and fiction essays encourage students to explore the definition of the word *hero*. Excellent material for class discussion. From the Icarus World Issues Series. ©1993

Redwall, Brian Jacques. In the glorious tradition of *Watership Down* comes the heart-soaring story of a wondrous quest to recover a legendary lost weapon and of a bumbling young apprentice monk named Matthias, mousekind's most unlikely hero. ©1990

Rescue: The Story of How Gentiles Saved Jews in the Holocaust, Milton Meltzer. Documents the efforts of the unsung heroes of the Holocaust—those gentiles who risked their own lives to save their Jewish friends and neighbors. Companion to *Never to Forget: The Jews of the Holocaust*. ©1991

Something for Joey, Richard Peck. While John Cappalletti was winning the Heisman Trophy, his brother Joey was suffering from leukemia. But John had a special medicine for Joey—touchdowns. ©1978

Witness, Karen Hesse. The year is 1924, and a small town in Vermont is falling under the influence of the Ku Klux Klan. Two girls, one black and the other Jewish, are among those who are no longer welcome. As the potential for violence increases, heroes—and villains—are revealed, and everyone in town is affected. ©2001

Acknowledgments

Text Credits CONTINUED FROM PAGE 2

"Excerpt from *Great Plains*" by Ian Frazier. Copyright © 1989 by Ian Frazier. Reprinted by permission of Farrar, Straus and Giroux, LLC.

Reprinted courtesy of *Sports Illustrated*: November 29, 1999, "Flying in the Face of the Fuhrer," by Phil Taylor, Copyright © 1999, Time Inc. All Rights Reserved.

"Hamish Mactavish Is Eating a Bus" by Gordon Korman. Copyright © 1997 by M. Jerry Weiss and Helen S. Weiss. From *One Experience to Another*, by M. Jerry Weiss and Helen S. Weiss. Reprinted by permission of St. Martin's Press, LLC.

"Hero's Return" from *Guests in the Promised Land* by Kristin Hunter. © 1968. Avon Books. Reprinted by permission.

"The Letter 'A'" by Christy Brown. Reprinted by permission of A.M. Heath & Co.

"Man in the Water" by Roger Rosenblatt. © 1982 Time Inc. Reprinted by permission.

"Older Run" from *Puppies, Dogs, and Blue Northers: Reflections on Being Raised by a Pack of Sled Dogs*. Copyright © 1996 by Gary Paulsen, reprinted with permission of Harcourt, Inc.

"Sir Bors Fights for a Lady", from *The Light Beyond the Forest* by Rosemary Sutcliff, copyright © 1979 by Rosemary Sutcliff. Used by permission of Dutton Children's Books, a division of Penguin Putnam Inc. Canadian rights by permission of David Higham Associates.

"A Song of Greatness" from *The Children Sing in the Far West* by Mary Austin. Copyright 1928 by Mary Austin, © renewed 1956 by Kenneth M. Chapman and Mary C. Wheelwright. Reprinted by permission of Houghton Mifflin Co. All rights reserved.

"The Teacher Who Changed My Life" by Nicholas Gage. Reprinted by permission of the author.

"Those Winter Sundays". Copyright © 1966 by Robert Hayden, from *Collected Poems of Robert Hayden* by Robert Hayden, edited by Frederick Glaysher. Used by permission of Liveright Publishing Corporation.

"Time for a Hero" by Brian M. Thomsen. Reprinted by permission of the author.

"Tough Alice" copyright © 1997 by Jane Yolen. First appeared in *Twelve Impossible Things Before Breakfast*, published by Harcourt Brace. Reprinted by permission of Curtis Brown, Ltd.

"Visible Ink" from *Blues: For All the Changes* by Nikki Giovanni. Copyright © 1999 by Nikki Giovanni. Reprinted by permission of HarperCollins Publishers, Inc.

"Who's the Greatest of All?" by Daniel Okrent. © 1998 Time Inc. Reprinted by permission.

"The Woodcutter's Story" by Nancy Schimmel. Reprinted by permission of the author.

Every reasonable effort has been made to properly acknowledge ownership of all material used. Any omissions or mistakes are not intentional and, if brought to the publisher's attention, will be corrected in future editions.

Photo and Art Credits Pages 3–5: Phoebe Hearst Museum of Anthropology, University of California at Berkeley. Page 9: © 2000 Mark Davison/Stone. Page 10: (top) © Bettmann/CORBIS (bottom) © The Stock Market/ Daniele Fiore 2000. Page 11: (top) © Bettmann/CORBIS (bottom) © 2000 Terry Vine/Stone. Page 13: © Michael Cardacino/Photonica. Pages 14, 21: Illustrations from Puppies, Dogs, and Blue Northers: Reflections on Being Raised by a Pack of Sled Dogs by Gary Paulsen, illustration copyright © 1996 by Ruth Paulsen, used with permission of Harcourt, Inc. Pages 22–23: © Jeanne Marklin/Contact Press Images. Page 22: © Bettmann/CORBIS. Page 26: Pablo Picasso: maquette for the cover of *Minotaure*. Paris (May 1933) Collage of pencil on paper, corrugated cardboard, silver foil, ribbon, wallpaper painted with gold paint and gouache, paper doily, burnt linen, leaves, tacks, and charcoal on wood, 19 1/8 x 16 1/8'' (48.5 x 41 cm). The Museum of Modern Art, New York. Gift of Mr. and Mrs. Alexandre P. Rosenberg. Photograph © 2000 The Museum of Modern Art, New York. Page 33: © 2000 Ferguson & Katzman/Stone. Pages 34–35: © Charles E. Rotkin/CORBIS. Page 34: Nicholas Gage. Page 37: Eddie Addams. Page 39: © Bettmann/CORBIS. Page 40: © Bettmann/CORBIS. Page 43: © Bettmann/CORBIS. Page 44: © Bettmann/CORBIS. Page 47: www.arttoday.com. Page 53: www.arttoday.com. Pages 54–55: © Bettmann/CORBIS. Page 56: Everett Collection. Page 63: © Knauer/Johnston/Photonica. Page 64: © Christie's Images Ltd. 2000. Page 69: © 2000 Stephen Studd/Stone. Page 70: U.S. Bureau of Public Roads. Page 71: © Bettmann/CORBIS. Page 79: Schlesinger Library, Radcliffe Institute, Harvard Library. Page 89: © Dynamic Duo Studio/SIS. Page 90: © Allan M. Burch. Page 99: © Kevin Horan/Stone. Page 100: (top) Reprinted by permission, Tribune Media Services, Orlando, Florida. Pages 100, 102–103: Mike Aspengren. Page 104: © Rick Berry, 1997. Page 114: AP/WIDE WORLD PHOTOS. Page 117: © Teofilo Olivieri/SIS. Pages 118–119: © Sandra Eisner/Photonica. Page 130: (top) © AFP/CORBIS (bottom) © Bettmann/CORBIS. Page 131: © Bettmann/CORBIS. Page 133: © Flip Schulke/CORBIS. Page 135: © 1991 Brenda Joysmith. Page 136: © Philippe Lardy.